The HIDDEN BRANCH

Mystery Novels by G. G. Vandagriff

Alex and Briggie Series

Cankered Roots

Of Deadly Descent

Tangled Roots

Poisoned Pedigree

Others

The Arthurian Omen: A Novel of Suspense

The Last Waltz: A Novel of Love and War

The HIDDEN BRANCH

A Mystery

G. G. VANDAGRIFF

SALT LAKE CITY, UTAH

Visit us at DeseretBook.com

Library of Congress Cataloging-in-Publication Data

Vandagriff, G. G.
The hidden branch / G.G. Vandagriff.
p. m.
Summary: Hired to find a murdered man's heirs, professional genealogist Alexandra Campbell and her sidekick, Briggie, are brought to the swanky beaches of Southern California and a community of Armenian relatives who all seem to be hiding a secret.
ISBN 978-1-60641-142-1 (paperbound)
1. Campbell, Alexandra (Fictitious character)—Fiction. 2. Poulson, Briggie (Fictitious character)—Fiction. 3. Women genealogists—Fiction. 4. Mormon women—Fiction. 5. Detective and mystery stories, American. I. Title.
PS3572.A427H53 2009
813'.54—dc22

2009026229

Printed in the United States of America
Edwards Brothers Incorporated, Ann Arbor, MI

10 9 8 7 6 5 4 3 2 1

In memory of my nephew

Scott Valentine Gibson

1976–1998

Our very own surfer, who has gone on before

A true asset to the kingdom of God

Acknowledgments

To my husband, David, who is always ready to help plot the next Alex and Briggie and to give me outrageous new ideas in the sticky patches. He is truly my co-creator. Huntington Beach was his idea. The Armenians were mine. What a combo!

To Rachel Ann Nunes for cheering me on when my energy flagged, for introducing me to the wonderful Storymakers, and for being my first reader when she had a very crowded schedule of her own.

To Alana Tompkins for insisting on another Alex and Briggie and for reading my manuscript when she should have been working on her Western Civ paper. I can't wait until Alana writes her first mystery—prepare to die of laughter, everyone!

As always, to Suzanne Brady for her enthusiasm for Alex and Briggie, her fine editing, and her deep friendship.

To JoAnn Jolley for editing this manuscript and for our new friendship.

And to Jana Erickson, product director at Deseret Book, for her cheerleading and her great efforts in producing and promoting my work.

A Word about Timing

This series was begun in 1993. We have advanced only one year in the characters' lives—to the summer of 1994. In those pre-Internet times, genealogical research was done the hard way.

Prologue

The burglar looked over the large Kansas City residence and wondered again how even the lucky son of a Turk could have such bad taste. The home was a mini castle with two turrets, wrought iron grills on the windows, phony Greek statues, and the ornate initials PM on the driveway. There were red pennants flying from the turrets. He felt personally injured by it. The neighbors probably thought Paul Mardian was nothing but a presumptuous Armenian. The man's father had been a garbage collector!

Yesterday he had watched with a powerful telescope from behind a hedge as Paul Mardian punched in the security code on the alarm outside his garage. Now, using that code, the burglar gained entrance to the four-car garage that housed Mardian's vintage Ferraris. Just moments ago, the man had taken the 1961 California Spyder out. Talk about sweet! Unfortunately, the burglar couldn't count hot-wiring cars among his talents.

After closing the garage door, he opened the door between the house and the garage and stepped into a laundry room, fitted out with a state-of-the-art washer and dryer. From there he went into a kitchen the size of a small barn. Copper pots hung from the ceiling. A granite-topped island stood in the center of the room, with one of those smooth-topped stoves and a built-in grill. Glass-fronted shelves displayed enough china and glassware for a dinner party of several dozen guests.

But what he was looking for wouldn't be in here. Proceeding down a long hall, he came to the door of the library. Was this where the treasures were kept? There! Mounted on the wall in glass cases were a couple of million dollars' worth of Armenian coins. Looking closer, he perceived that they were from the time of Tigranes II the Great—about 100 B.C. Tigranes the Great. His royal ancestor. The natural right of ownership burned inside him.

He had read recently that he actually carried part of his ancestors within him. Nothing as commonplace as DNA, but actual molecules in his cells that were passed from generation to generation. This feeling of ownership must have stemmed from the fact that Tigranes the Great was alive inside him, having passed through all of his ancestors down to him.

He himself had journeyed to his homeland once it had been freed from Soviet domination, searching for something, anything, that had survived the Armenian Holocaust. He had found little. Everything had been smashed and burned and destroyed by the Turks and Soviets.

Yet here before him a vast collection glittered. It would be a legacy *he,* the descendant of Tigranes, could leave that would empower Armenians everywhere. They would understand that they had descended from a culturally distinct and glorious people they could be proud of. They could push for recognition in the world as a people who had been tragic victims of genocide. He cursed the Turks for their ruin of Armenia and often dreamt terrible scenes from the

Holocaust, though he had been born in America as part of the great Armenian Diaspora. But Armenians were blessed with the great gift of contriving and surviving, and after only eighty years in the New World, they were carving out their place.

Removing the artifacts from their cases was time-consuming but lovingly accomplished. He had brought a box and a roll of cotton in which to wrap each precious item. It was an ennobling experience just to have them in his hands, and he had to force himself to go faster. Here was something concrete that still existed, calling to the voices in his blood.

Then he heard the unmistakable sound of the garage door opening. What was this? Mardian was back already?

If he entered this room, he would immediately see there was a burglary in progress. Quickly surveying the library, the intruder's eyes paused on the long velvet drapes. That's where burglars always hid in the movies. He slipped behind them, leaving the treasures in the open.

Mardian strode into the room moments later. Through the crack in the drapes, the burglar could see him. The swarthy fifty-year-old man's eyes went immediately to the wall that was almost stripped of its treasures. Then he saw the open box on the floor. Coolly, he went to his desk and took a huge automatic pistol out of the top drawer.

"I know you're here," he bellowed in his deep bass voice. "I'm going to find you and put a bullet through your kneecap. Only then will I call the police. You're one of *them,* aren't you? It's a good thing I haven't taken the new will to Grinnell. It will be an easy thing to tear up the draft."

Looking behind the door and seeing no one, he strode from the room. The burglar took up a heavy brass statuette of some Greek god and followed him out of the office.

Chapter One

The telephone awakened Alexandra Campbell at six A.M. She had no idea that moment signaled the beginning of one of those fiery trials after which you are never the same. In the future, she would count time forward from that day for the rest of her life. On that morning, however, she only knew that there was just one person who would dare call her at such an hour.

"Briggie!" she greeted her business partner and mentor. "What in the world is so important?" Arrayed in her customary nightwear—her fiancé's Christ Church College crew shirt—she vaguely noted that the persistent Kansas City humidity had not broken overnight.

"I need you, Alex. I'm having a crisis."

Briggie? Crisis? The words didn't go together. This friend, who had rescued her from the grief over her husband's death and then loved her into the gospel, was not your typical little old lady. Spring days found her down in the Ozarks fishing for trout, and summer days cheering from the cheap seats at the Kansas City Royals ballpark.

Fall meant one thing: hunting for whitetails with her well-worn deer rifle. Gruff and gutsy, her friend was not the sort to have angst.

"I'll be there in half an hour," Alex told her, calculating that she could shower and dress in ten minutes. Her Westport apartment was twenty minutes from Briggie's big white house in Independence.

"Thanks, I don't need to see you, but just answer me this," Briggie said. "Is it required that you wear a bikini when you learn to surf? I mean, do you think I'd stand out too much if I didn't?"

After the initial shock of picturing the short and rounded Brighamina Poulson, mother of nine and grandmother of twenty-five, cutting across the waves in a hot pink bikini, laughter bubbled up through her. "Briggie," she said, "everyone has a wet suit now. So you can wear your bikini underneath and still keep your temple recommend. But where is your surfing debut supposed to take place?"

"Could you be ready to go to California this afternoon?" This time there was a plaintive note in her voice.

"California?" What was this? Unfortunately, in addition to her virtues, her colleague was known for her harebrained schemes.

"I need a chaperone."

Alex rolled her eyes. At sixty-something (Briggie was coy about her age), she needed a chaperone?

"Good grief, Briggie, spit it out. What's going on?"

"Well . . . I haven't mentioned it before, because I thought it was sort of ridiculous and would die a natural death, but Richard has asked me to marry him, of all things . . ."

"Briggie!" Now Alex *was* shocked. Richard was a sedate, wealthy estate lawyer from the ritzy part of Kansas City who brought their genealogical research company much of its business. He had shown nothing but disdain for Briggie's deer rifle, the Royals, and her general way of life. The fact that they disagreed on almost every issue had not prevented them from leading one another into danger on several of RootSearch, Inc.'s investigations that had turned murderous.

"I'm not falling for his line, so don't worry, but things are kinda awkward. He's invited me to this place called 'Surf City.' He has to go meet some heirs and wants my help to find them. We're supposed to leave this afternoon, and I've got cold feet."

Very suspicious behavior for Richard, Alex agreed. "Why wasn't I invited? He knows we work as a team."

Here Briggie seemed to hesitate. "Well . . . aren't you and Charles taking that trip to the East Coast?"

"You know that isn't until next week. There's something else. What is it? Are you afraid he'll only pay for a single room in some posh hotel?"

"Well . . . he might actually try that if we weren't taking Marigny with us. He wants her to have a little vacation. Apparently, this beach is really spectacular. It's where all the surfers hang out, and she's never seen the ocean." Marigny was Richard's sixteen-year-old granddaughter.

"So what's the problem? Why hasn't he asked both of us?"

"It's Marigny," Briggie finally admitted. "She doesn't want you to come."

Alex was stunned. She plunked down into her desk chair, looking blankly at the office that appeared as if it had been visited by Dorothy's tornado. "She doesn't like me anymore? Why?"

Briggie sighed gustily. "I'm sure it'll pass, Alex, but she's really upset about your engagement. I didn't stop to think about it before, but she was certain you were going to marry her dad."

Daniel. Richard's son had helped Alex out of her gloom, waiting patiently for her to stop grieving over Stewart's death. However, on a case that took her to Oxford, England, she had met Charles—a blond, classically featured British bachelor—who had swept her off her feet, very much against her will. She had only decided to marry Charles for sure last month, and Daniel was not happy about it. She really couldn't blame him. It had been a difficult decision for her.

"Well," Alex said after vacillating a moment, "I'm sure Richard will behave himself in front of his granddaughter."

"It's not that, exactly," Briggie said. "Marigny would be thrilled if Richard and I got married, so she promotes it every chance she gets. It's two against one."

"So you need me to even out the numbers? What makes you think I wouldn't want you to marry Richard? I think you're good for the old stuffed shirt. Remember when you two broke into Johnny's love nest looking for those letters, and Richard was only concerned about the tear in his new trousers? Daniel and I never laughed so hard."

"Alex, you're forgetting the Church. I am sealed to my Ned, and I would never get married again to someone who wasn't a member. We wouldn't get along."

"Oh . . . yeah. I was kind of forgetting. I'm so new at this." She had been baptized into The Church of Jesus Christ of Latter-day Saints only a year and a half before. "Well, if you're really serious, I'll give Charles a call and see if he'd rather take a vacation to the West Coast and see a different side of America. They sure don't have a surfing culture in England."

"I want to get the two of you on our flight, so get back to me right away, okay?" Briggie sounded anxious. Alex wondered if her friend was a little afraid of being almost alone with Richard. Was she worried she might give in to his importuning?

Before she called Charles, Alex made a pot of peppermint tea in the little Ainsley china teapot he had given her, allowing herself time to wake up properly. Carrying her tea and holding the portable phone between her shoulder and ear, she walked into the bedroom where she had just hung the oval beveled mirror Charles had bought at auction for their future home. Looking at her riot of black ringlets and her pale white skin, almost blue under the eyes, she thought that she could use a little California sun. Growing up by the lake in Chicago, she had always had a tan in the summertime. Her father and grandfather had taken her out on the boat before all the problems that crippled them into a dysfunctional family. She was grateful that she had her good memories back now that all the secrets had been aired.

Dialing Charles's number in Chicago, she marveled, as she did every day of her new life, that this forty-six–year-old bachelor ever could have come to love her. She was thankful for the teapot, the mirror, and a small snapshot of the two of them, Charles standing behind with his arms around her shoulders and his face next to hers. For so long this apartment had housed her grief and anger at Stewart's death, and it was wonderful to be filling it with happy things from her new love.

"Alex, I'm always happy to hear from you, darling, but whatever possessed you to call so early?" her fiancé asked with unaccustomed grumpiness.

"I'm sorry, Charles. It's just that Briggie is having a crisis. She needs us to fly to California with her today. Can you get away?"

"*Briggie* is having a crisis?"

"Richard wants to marry her, and he's spiriting her away to Surf City to plead his case."

Charles choked on a laugh. "Surely you're kidding. Is there really such a place? And Briggie and Richard *married?* With the antics those two get up to, he'd probably be disbarred before they celebrated their first anniversary."

Alex giggled, a thing she'd found herself doing lately, now that her angst-driven years seemed to be behind her. "I know. It's pretty terrifying to think about. I think she's afraid she'll give in, so she wants us to chaperone."

Charles chuckled. "Well, this I have to see. I wonder what stuffy old Richard's beachwear will be?"

"He did wear Levi's on our last case, remember. That's more than you did."

"Is there really such a place as Surf City?"

"In California, anything's possible, but I think she means Huntington Beach. Surf City is its nickname. It's supposed to be a fun place. I'm hoping to get a tan."

"You'll look just like a little sapphire-eyed gypsy," her fiancé teased.

"What do you look like with a tan?"

"Can't say I've ever had one. Remember, I grew up in a beastly climate. When I rowed, it was always raining."

"Well, I hope you don't freckle. It would certainly ruin the GQ image."

"Would it? Then I hope devoutly that I will freckle, so I can see if you're only marrying me for my looks."

"More like I'm going to have to handcuff you to me to make sure you don't get carried off by bevies of bikini beauties," Alex said. "On second thought, I don't dare risk it. You can't come, Charles. You'll just have to stay in Chicago and oversee our probate, like the good guy you are." Charles was actually a third cousin with a large family in England who were coheirs to Alex's family's meatpacking fortune.

"I can't possibly let Briggie down, Alex. And I wouldn't miss a chance to experience the culture of Surf City. Besides, I need to see you. There's something we probably should discuss, much as I dread it."

"What is it?" she asked, alarmed.

"Not something to hash out over the telephone. And there's no reason I can't take a holiday. I was planning to take the week off next week anyway, for our trip east. The probate is well in hand. Everything is sailing on smoothly at our meat plant under the fellow who's hoping to buy it. Cows are turning into hamburgers at an ever quickening pace."

What could he have to tell her? Alex tried to lighten the tone once more. "Just so you know, I don't wear bikinis."

"How unfortunate," he said with a sigh. "On what pretext is Richard spiriting Briggie away? I thought it was impossible to get her out of Kansas City during baseball season."

"It's a new case. I don't know any details."

"It is rather odd that he didn't ask you along as well, then."

"He's taking Marigny—you know, Daniel's daughter. She apparently hates me now because I'm marrying you instead of her father."

"Then I must come. Sixteen-year-old girls are apt to be emotionally unpredictable. You could be in danger, darling."

Alex phoned Briggie to report that Charles was flying in from Chicago as soon as he could. Their flight from Kansas City to Orange County was to leave at three o'clock.

"Bring the documents in your carry-on, Briggs, so I can look them over on the plane."

"Richard's bringing them. Thanks for coming, kiddo."

Meanwhile, deep inside, a worm of worry had started. What would Charles have to tell her that could make him so reluctant?

Chapter Two

Charles arrived at Alex's apartment via the fire escape (the elevator in the Baltimore Apartments was permanently out of order) just as she was finishing her packing. Upon answering the door, she was swept off her feet and twirled around as he planted kisses all over her face. As usual, his presence lifted her heart. Before Charles, it had been numb, encased in a protective shield for many years, even during her ten-year marriage. Before Charles, she hadn't known what it was to trust.

"Charles! Put me down for heaven's sake! I want to kiss you properly!"

Ignoring her plea, he carried her over the threshold, leaving his suitcase on the fire escape. "You know, I've always liked your place," he said, his tone oddly nostalgic as he carried her into the living room and set her on her feet. He was looking around at her white Bauhaus furniture, cherrywood Parsons table, imitation Persian rug, and Stewart's photographic posters she had framed on her walls. They depicted European capitals and had been his last commission before the plane crash that had killed him and pitched her into a depression so profound she had wished she were dead. "Stewart was one heck of a photographer," Charles said. "He always had such an unusual perspective, and the things he did with light were pure genius."

"I don't know if Stewart would have liked you," she said, poking him in the ribs. "He took being a Scot very seriously." For the first time, she noticed the dark circles under his eyes. They didn't go with his Englishman-on-holiday clothes—lightweight trousers, a crisp blue and white striped shirt, and canvas rope-soled shoes. "But he would probably have wanted you to model for him."

"I never knew he did portraits."

"Well, you would have had to take most of your clothes off to show your rowing muscles."

He kissed her thoroughly on the lips. "I guess on this little beach jaunt of ours, you're going to get to see them, if they haven't atrophied completely."

"Umm," she said, initiating another kiss so heated, she knew they'd better get out of the apartment fast.

Briggie and Richard were at the gate by the time Charles and Alex arrived. Their flight was already boarding.

"Alex!" Briggie exclaimed. "Charles! I was sure you were going to miss the plane." Because it was summer, she had forsaken her customary sweats for a bright blue Kansas City Royals jersey with George Brett's uniform number on the back and white polyester pants. She carried only a duffle that Alex was sure was stuffed with similar outfits. Her short white hair was spiked up, not intentionally but because she had been running her fingers through it, as usual.

Suave, sophisticated Richard with his gorgeous white mane stood beside her, briefcase in hand, dressed in a light summer suit and a baby blue shirt. Sitting on a chair behind all of them sat Marigny Grinnell, his granddaughter, with way too much makeup on her young face and her red ringlets confined by a rubber band on top of her head. Alex remembered that Daniel had said she was going through a femme fatale stage. The girl was in an obvious pout. As her grandfather shook hands with Alex and Charles, she pointedly refused to greet them.

Minutes later, they were all boarding the plane. Briggie and Alex sat next to each other in first class, with Richard on the aisle seat across from them, so they could discuss the case. Charles and Marigny sat behind Richard, and Alex had absolutely no doubt that by the end of the flight Charles would have charmed her out of her sulk. He was very, very good at that sort of thing.

As soon as they were airborne, Richard took a fat file from his briefcase and handed it to Briggie. "This is what I've got. Paul Mardian was extremely wealthy, and I've put everything together in one file in case it has relevance. He had three Ferraris, of all things."

Alex opened the file and stared at the first paper. "Billionaire Murdered in Sunset Drive Mansion," read the headline of the *Kansas City Star.* It was dated two weeks before. "You didn't tell us he was murdered!" she exclaimed. "How could you forget a little detail like that?"

"Yeah." Briggie scowled at the headline. "Why on earth didn't you mention it, Richard? It could have a huge bearing on what we find. You of all people know that murderers can't benefit from their victim's death."

Richard shrugged. "I knew it would raise a red flag with you two." He shook his head. "You probably could have helped him. He was a bit quirky. In the last couple of years, he became obsessed with his Armenian heritage. Then he visited me and told me he had pancreatic cancer, and while he still could, he was going to visit Ellis Island to look at his grandfather's immigration records. That's how he found out that his grandfather had another son older than Paul's father, I guess, but that's the last time I saw him. According to those papers with the handwritten will I found in his desk, he hired a genealogist to find out what happened to the other son. Apparently there's a huge crew of his progeny in Huntington Beach. It's all in there." The lawyer smiled grimly. "That handwritten will must be the draft he said he was going to bring to me, but he signed it, so it's legal. Good thing I went looking for it."

"It's not like you to be so naïve, Richard," Briggie scolded. "If those California cousins were his only heirs, how do you know they didn't kill him?"

"Maybe you're right," Richard said thoughtfully, and his eyes took on the gleam that Alex had come to dread. When associated with Briggie on a case that involved skulduggery of any kind, the two of them were apt to shuck their law-abiding, middle-aged shells and become desperados. "I assumed it was a break-in that went wrong. That's what the police think. A bunch of valuable antiquities are missing."

"They don't have the data you do! I'm truly ashamed of you, Richard," Briggie told him. "What has happened to your common sense?"

He looked disgruntled, and with his customary bark that he usually moderated only in Briggie's presence, he ordered a bottle of bourbon from the flight attendant. Briggie sniffed and turned her air vent pointedly in his direction, presumably to dispel the bourbon fumes.

"Where's this confounded will?" she demanded querulously. Alex had never known Richard to drink liquor in their presence before.

As Briggie paged through the file, Alex looked back at Charles. He was ordering a Shirley Temple for Marigny. She appeared much more like the teenager Alex was accustomed to seeing. How was her father taking this little expedition? Daniel had loved going sleuthing with them in the past. Did he feel left out? Alex became aware of a twinge of regret. Though she had chosen not to marry him, Daniel was like family to her. He and Briggie had seen her through many a rocky time before Charles came on the scene. That was one of the reasons she had chosen not to marry him—because that grieving, angst-driven Alex wasn't who she really was. The woman Charles had fallen in love with was competent and self-assured, not haunted by the specters of way too many tragedies. But the fact remained that Daniel loved her in spite of all her flaws and weaknesses. There would always be a tie between them, even when she married Charles. Daniel thought he was her dragonslayer. Charles would never presume that she needed one.

Briggie was squinting at an illegible scrawl on a piece of yellow legal paper. "You'd sure think this Paul Mardian would have more sense," she said. "Richard made him a perfectly good will, and he goes and scraps it and comes up with this handwritten gobbledygook that no one can possibly read. And it's not even a trust! Whoever inherits is going to have to pay out a bunch of money in taxes."

"Who was the legatee under the first will?"

"His trust, which was to be divided up between eight or so charities. This one leaves everything to the heirs of Vazken Mardian, to be divided equally among them. I'm assuming Vazken was the long-lost uncle he found in the Ellis Island records. But there are so many cross-outs in all different colors of ink! I can barely read it." Absorbed, she finally said, "He was fixated on the Armenian genocide. Obviously, the common grandfather came over to this country to escape the Turks."

Briggie lifted the will, displaying the first of many complicated-looking documents. "Richard told me that this Paul Mardian invented the pop-top can. This is the patent. Can you imagine the fortune he must have made? Geesh."

"With that much money involved, I'm anxious to read that

article about his murder. I'll do that while you try to make something of that will."

Briggie nodded shortly and handed Alex the clipping from *The Kansas City Star.* The body of the article read:

Prominent Kansas City inventor Paul Mardian was found murdered at his Sunset Avenue home on Thursday, leaving behind no immediate family, his wife, Jane, and son, Robert, having died in 1985. The deceased was a well-known Kansas City citizen and benefactor, as well as the inventor of the pop-top can.

The police are calling the murder the result of an interrupted robbery. Mardian collected ancient artifacts, valued at several million dollars, that were missing when his cleaning service found the body. The medical examiner has determined that Mardian died from a blunt force trauma to the head. Mardian was carrying a handgun when someone apparently struck him from behind. The gun had not been fired.

A description of the stolen artifacts was obtained from Mardian's insurance company and is being circulated throughout this country by the FBI, as well as abroad by Interpol.

The Mardians are a great American success story, as Paul Mardian was fond of telling people. In a 1988 interview upon the dedication of the Mardian Amphitheater, he related his family saga. In 1915 Ayk Abaven Mardian escaped the Turkish genocide of his people that resulted in the death of more than one million Armenians, and worked his way to America with his wife, Baydzar. They remained in New York only a few years before relocating to Chicago, where Ayk Mardian labored at Lakeland Steel. His son, Hamazasb Mardian, married Ramela Agajanian, who died giving birth to Paul. Hamazasb had a large waste collection business and was prominent in the Armenian community of Chicago.

After his father's death in 1980, Paul Mardian and his wife, Jane Sarkesian Mardian, moved to Kansas City to be near his wife's elderly parents. The inventor used his extensive wealth to benefit the University of

Missouri at Kansas City and build the Mardian Amphitheater. Services will be held at the Apostolic Armenian Church Friday at ten o'clock. The service is open to the public.

Alex used her notebook to sketch the descendancy chart of Ayk Abaven Mardian.

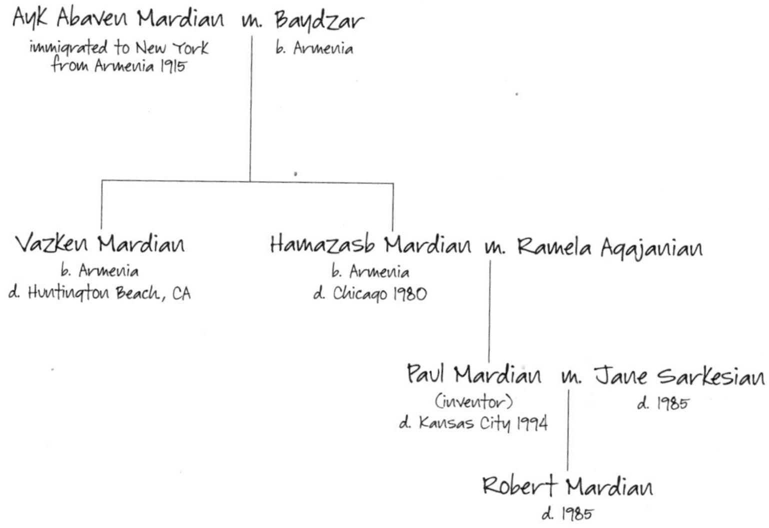

Briggie whistled. "Poor guy died only two weeks ago. Richard went to the funeral. Good thing he signed this will. He was probably superstitious. There's some correspondence attached between him and the genealogist about this clan of Mardians living in Huntington Beach, where his uncle Vazken died. In the will, he left his fortune to Vazken's descendants." The older woman shook her head. "I wonder if he ever met his cousins, or whether he was too sick. This letter is dated just a month ago." Reading further, she said, "But maybe he did. His historic artifacts were meant to go to the Apostolic Armenian Church in Huntington Beach. A wing was to be built to house them. He left a separate provision for it."

"So," Alex reasoned, "it sounds like the antiquities must have been Armenian."

"What did you learn in the article?" Briggie asked.

"Well, apparently Paul was fond of telling everyone that his family was an American success story. According to this, his father Hamazasb was the only son of his grandfather. The reporter who wrote it had no knowledge of this Vazken's family."

"There must have been a family tiff in the old days. Vazken took off. Maybe for California. Maybe before Paul was born," Briggie surmised.

"Must have been a pretty serious family tiff if Paul didn't even know he had an uncle!"

"Armenians are Middle Easterners, remember. Family loyalty is extremely important," Briggie said. "Vazken must have crossed his father somehow."

Alex was looking at the laser-printed stationery of the letter from the genealogist. "Paul was sure obsessed with his heritage. Look! The genealogist was even an Armenian—Leon Mugerian."

"Well, that makes sense. He was probably an expert on Armenian families."

At that moment, the flight attendant came by with their meals—chicken Cordon Bleu, rice pilaf, peas, and a hard roll. For dessert there was a rich square of chocolate cake.

"Ah, bless Paul Mardian's estate for the first class tickets!" Briggie murmured before she tucked into the meal.

"So, ladies, what did you make of that?" Richard asked, seeming to have recovered his temper.

"A solid motive for murder," Briggie told him. "The antiquities that were stolen were worth millions. They were to go to a church in Huntington Beach instead of the relatives. Have you tried to get in touch with this genealogist to see if Mardian ever met his family there?"

"The phone number had been disconnected. The address was in a run-down part of town, and there was no one by that name living or working there. That letter from him says he saw an ad Paul placed in some publication called *Binding Hearts.*"

"And you didn't find that suspicious?" Briggie asked. "Good grief, Richard, what has happened to your instincts? He was probably posing as a genealogist! I'll bet he was one of Paul Mardian's long-lost cousins who saw the ad! If only you had known what your client was looking for, you could have put him in touch with us. Maybe the bourbon was clouding your judgment."

"Well, now, Brighamina, don't you go blaming me," Richard said in an obvious huff. "The last time I spoke to the man, he was on his way to Ellis Island."

"Mugerian, Mardian. Not much difference." Briggie mumbled.

"I'd say your scenario was a little bit of a long shot," Richard said with a gusty sigh. "His murderer really could have been anyone who knew about the loot. I'll bet you anything he had people in to see it all the time. He was obviously very proud of it."

Alex glanced back at Charles and was surprised to see him studying her. His countenance was uncharacteristically solemn. *What in heaven's name was wrong?*

Chapter Three

They arrived at John Wayne International Airport right at rush hour. Alex made sure she had a seat next to Charles in the minivan that Richard had reserved for them. Taking his long-fingered hand in hers, she leaned over and whispered in his ear, "Has something happened? You look so sad!"

"Not now, darling. We'll discuss it later, when we're alone."

Alex's anxiety, never far from the surface, increased. It wasn't helped by Briggie and Richard's sniping in the front seat over the map's directions. By the time they arrived at the beautiful Hyatt Regency, built in mission style and surrounded by palm trees just across the highway from the ocean, she was in no mood to appreciate it. Questions were chasing through her mind. *Was Charles having second thoughts? Or had someone in his family died? No. Surely, if that were it, he'd be on his way to England.*

She and Briggie were given a room on the third floor with a little wrought iron balcony that was ideal for watching the blue-green ocean. Alex had never seen the Pacific from this continent. She and

Stewart had traveled on photography expeditions through the Hawaiian Islands and many beauty spots in the South Pacific, but she had never been to California. It was a relief to feel the cool ocean breeze after the unrelenting Midwestern humidity. Huntington Beach reminded her a little of Hawaii with its palm trees and holiday atmosphere. An ache tugged at her heart. It was there that she and Stewart had conceived Megan, the daughter she had borne prematurely in the trauma following Stewart's death. The event was so terrible that she had actually blocked it from her memory until last month. The grief was still fresh and raw, only mitigated by the fact that she and Charles were planning to have a family.

There have been so many traumas. My banishment by my parents, Stewart's and Megan's tragic deaths, my father's murder, my mother's alcoholism. But Charles has helped me to put them firmly in the past, loving me with his whole heart. Or is that an illusion? Is he going to leave me now?

Mentally slapping herself, she went inside and surveyed the luxurious suite. She was a new Alex who didn't look for abandonment around every corner. Right?

Everything around her combined to soothe her back into her confident persona—sand-hued walls, ocean-colored bedspread, shrimp pink upholstered furniture. She could take refuge from Briggie's snores in the pull-out bed in the sitting room. Alex began to unpack her jeans, T-shirts, her Speedo bathing suit, some gauzy skirts, and her sandals. She was also glad that Marigny hadn't been put in with them. The girl hadn't said a word to Alex all the way from the airport, though she had frequently tossed coquettish remarks over her shoulder at Charles. Preoccupied, Alex hadn't paid any attention, noting only that Charles's grip on her hand was tighter than usual during the entire ride.

Thinking she might catch him alone before dinner, Alex took her key and left Briggie singing "She'll be comin' round the mountain" in the shower. Charles did not answer her knock. Perhaps he was out on his balcony. Frustrated, she went back to her room and called him. He didn't pick up.

So much for that. Well, she had a job to do. Taking the thick Huntington Beach telephone book out from under the nightstand, she looked up Mardians. There was a short list:

Henry Mardian
Thomas Mardian
Vaz Mardian's Surfboards Unlimited

As she had suspected, it would have been easy for Richard to find them. This trip was clearly a boondoggle at Paul Mardian's expense.

At that moment, there was a knock at the door. To Alex's surprise, it was Marigny, who stood looking at her sandaled feet with their four toe rings. She had changed to shorts and a turquoise blouse with its tails tied at her slim waist.

"Why aren't you going to marry my dad?" she blurted. "Can't you see that Charles is one big phony?"

Alex drew the girl in out of the hall and sat her down on the couch. "We need to have a little talk, Marigny." She opened the small refrigerator. "Would you like juice or something?"

The girl shook her head. Alex took out a can of ginger ale and poured it into a glass she found in the kitchenette, trying to think of what to say. Finally, she seated herself beside the girl.

"I love your dad a lot, Marigny. He's like family to me. Like you are. Like Briggie and your grandfather are. You'll always be part of my life."

"But we're *not* family unless you marry my dad, and Briggie marries Grandpa."

"I can understand how much you want a family, honey. When I

was eighteen, my parents sent me away to Paris and told me not to come home. It was awful. I have never been so lonely or felt so abandoned in my life."

After a silent moment, Marigny looked up, her heavily mascared eyes full of tears. "I never knew that! How awful!" She looked down at her shorts and picked at a side seam. "My mom left when I was only ten. But at least I have Dad, even if we fight all the time. I don't think he loves me as much as Grandpa does."

"If anything, he loves you more. But your dad has responsibility for you. He doesn't want to see you hurt or make decisions you might regret later. Grandparents don't discipline. They just love you for who you are. And your dad's a shrink, which makes it worse. He can see things you don't want him to."

Marigny appeared to be absorbing this. "Is that why you won't marry him?"

Giving what she hoped was a genuine laugh, she said, "It's not very comfortable to have someone walking around in your head, is it?" That had indeed been a major barrier to a marital relationship with Daniel. "But that's not it. I love Charles in a different way, Marigny. He's not a phony. His charm is just part of him, like being British. I think your dad sort of thinks of me as a patient. Charles sees the real me, like I was before my husband was killed in a plane crash."

Marigny said in a small voice, "Dad told me it was terrorists."

Alex studied the girl's piquant face. It was so delicate—the perfect mouth, the tiny tip-tilted nose, and the velvety brown eyes. It occurred to her for the first time that Daniel's wife must have been a pretty woman. But the drama queen attitude did not suit Marigny. Nor did heavy makeup. "That's right, and it was awful. Then Briggie came to Scotland where I lived. I didn't even know her, but she rescued me. She was there on a genealogy trip. That's how I became a genealogist."

"Genealogy is pretty cool. It's like detective work. I loved helping you with that last case. Can I help you with this one?" With Alex's explanations, she had dropped her ruefulness, and turned into the eager teenager Alex knew.

She smiled. "Sure, Marigny. Maybe there's someone in your generation you can get to be friends with. Then you can kind of go undercover and find out stuff."

Briggie walked into the sitting room in a fresh blue button-down shirt that Alex recognized as her bowling shirt. On the back it had a huge embroidered tiger. Marigny grinned at the sight of her.

"Well, folks, what're we doing for dinner?"

By common consent, the company chose to walk out on the pier and eat at the legendary Ruby's, a diner where they could watch the sunset. Charles had returned from what turned out to have been a brisk walk reconnoitering the area. Ruby's was his idea. "Seems to be a bit of an institution," he explained. "The pier's been torn down by storms, but they always resurrect Ruby's."

As they walked the length of the pier to their destination, Alex held Charles's hand and breathed in lungfuls of sea air. Gulls flapped around the men and women who leaned on the pier, lazily watching their fishing lines. Briggie eyed the fishing gear with semiprofessional interest. There were shops with postcards, T-shirts, hats, and other paraphernalia advertising "Surf City."

When they reached Ruby's, a small diner with huge windows looking north, south, and east, all the booths were filled, so Alex's group sat at the counter. She was rather surprised by Charles's choice. He was a gourmet and didn't consider fries and hamburgers a real meal. Alex did.

"I'll have your guacamole burger with fries and a chocolate

shake," she said to the waitress who was dressed in a red and white fifties-style dress, apron, and cap. To her amusement, Marigny copied her order. Richard was sniffing at the menu. Charles ordered a cobb salad with bleu cheese dressing and lemonade. Briggie wanted the cheeseburger with fries and an Oreo milkshake with extra Oreos. Finally, Richard ordered a salad.

"This is a kid's place, Charles," he complained.

"Atmosphere," Charles explained. "Nothing like this in Kansas City. Watch those seagulls dive for fish. Fantastic! Briggie, you'll have to hire a rod. Did you see all the people fishing off the pier?"

"Maybe," Briggie said. "But I've been thinking. Much as I hate to admit it, I may be a little on the old side for a surfboard, but in the airline magazine I read about something called a boogie board that sounds like my style."

Richard snorted. "That, Brighamina, I've got to see."

"It wouldn't hurt you to give it a try, Mr. Smarty Pants," she replied. "It might be a way to loosen you up without alcohol."

Sensing a quarrel (why in the world did Richard want to marry Briggie, anyway?), Alex said, "I looked up Mardians in the Huntington Beach phone book. To start with, we have Vaz, who owns a surfboard shop. I'm assuming he's Paul Mardian's cousin once removed, named after Paul's grandfather Vazken, if he's the age to be into surfing. There's Thomas, and Henry as well."

"Did you get the addresses?" Briggie asked.

"Yes. I'm sure the surfboard shop is open late, so we can do a little sleuthing after dinner."

"Then I can buy my boogie board," said her cohort. "Good idea, Alex."

Vaz Mardian's Surfboards Unlimited was on the main drag—a continuation of the pier. The street was clogged with bicycles, people sitting at outdoor tables eating and drinking, as well as three breakdancers performing for the patrons. Vaz Mardian's shop had a gaudy exterior with graffiti-like art depicting a surfer on an enormous wave. The inside was crowded with tanned, blond surfers buying all manner of surfing paraphernalia. Alex guessed that it must be a sort of surfers cult locale. There were Surf City T-shirts in all sizes from six months to XXX Large. They all had a logo on the back, "I met Vaz," with the spiky signature of Vazken Mardian below.

Vaz must be some kind of surfing legend. There were pictures of Vaz with trophies on the walls. Alex looked at the surfboards in all colors and sizes, smaller boards that she took to be boogie boards, straps whose function Alex couldn't guess, wet suits from small to large, goggles, and fins.

Briggie commenced picking over the wet suits, Richard standing over her. "You want one in royal blue, I suppose," he said. Richard was an obdurate St. Louis Cardinals baseball fan, a thorn in their relationship from the very beginning.

Marigny was put out that they didn't seem to carry bikinis, but she started browsing the T-shirts. Charles and Alex made their way to the back of the store, where one of the handsomest youths Alex had ever seen was ringing up sales. His jet black hair was curly and almost long enough to brush his shoulders. His baby blue eyes stood out in his finely sculpted brown face. Attractively one-sided, his smile showed very white, straight teeth. This was one attractive Armenian. Alex braced herself for the moment when Marigny spotted him. Before she could do so, Alex walked up to him and asked, "Are you Vazken Mardian's son?"

"I'm Benji, the nephew," he said. "You need to see my uncle?"

"If he's here," Alex said.

"Sure. Just let me ring up this sale, and I'll get him." He flashed his trademark grin at the blonde, pony-tailed beauty he was helping.

The man who came out from the back of the store introduced

himself as Vaz Mardian. He was another handsome specimen, closer to Alex's age. His hair was long, a gold earring peeked from his earlobe, and he wore a Hawaiian shirt in blue-green that matched his eyes. Richard was in trouble. Even at her age, Briggie was sure to develop a crush on this man!

"I'm Alex Campbell, and this is my fiancé, Charles Lamb. Can we go for a little stroll? I'm here to see you on business."

The man cocked his head. "What're you selling?" he asked sharply.

"It's family business," she clarified.

"Is my family okay? Are you a cop?" The man looked her up and down, seemingly oblivious to Charles standing next to her.

"No, nothing like that. I'm a genealogist."

"Genealogist?" Vaz looked blank.

"I trace family trees. Right now I'm working on yours."

"Why?" His eyes narrowed in suspicion.

"We'd rather talk to you alone," Alex temporized. "It's sort of noisy in here."

Vaz grinned. "Yeah, just the way we like it. Let's go down the street for an espresso."

He came out from behind the counter, and Charles and Alex followed him out of the store to the sidewalk café they had passed—Costa Rica Coffee. It had a darkened interior that reminded Alex of an English pub, but the white outside tables with their green and white umbrellas were pure California beach style. Right now, they were just in time to enjoy a vermilion sunset with the pier silhouetted black against it.

"I'll go in and order," Charles said. "What can I get for you, Mr. Mardian?"

"Vaz. I'll have a double latte with whipped cream."

"Alex?" Charles asked.

"A peppermint steamer," she answered. "You're allowed. It's just steamed milk with flavoring." Charles, recently baptized, was still getting used to living without coffee and tea. "Oh, and the chocolate chip cookies look good on this little menu thing. Could I have one of those, too?"

"I'll grab one for Briggie, while I'm at it," he said with a grin.

After her fiancé had entered the espresso bar, Alex turned to Vaz. "We don't mean to be mysterious, but are you descended from Vazken Mardian?"

The man was clearly taken aback. "Yeah. He was my grandfather."

"I suppose you can prove it, if necessary?"

"Why?"

"Well, it seems you had a great-uncle you probably never heard of. I'm not sure I'm pronouncing it right, but his name was Hamazasb Mardian. His son, Paul, just died and left everything to your grandfather's descendants."

Vaz leaned back in his wrought iron chair and stroked his upper lip with his forefinger. "Intriguing. I didn't know there were any other Mardians around. He didn't have any family?"

At that moment, Charles arrived with their drinks on a tray. Alex took hers and tentatively sipped it. Mistake. It was too hot.

"No. And, incidentally, he was murdered. From your reaction, I gather he was never in touch with you or your family?" she asked.

"Murdered? How?" Vaz was leaning forward now, studying her face as though he could read deception there. His forthright gaze made her uncomfortable. A thought flew into her head. *He could be the murderer. He could have posed as Mugerian, and Paul wouldn't have known the difference.*

"I'm not exactly sure. Someone was robbing him, and he interrupted." She waited a moment while he stroked his lip again and then asked her question once more. "Did he come here? Did you meet him?"

"No. He never came. At least, I never met him or heard about him, and we're about as tightly knit a family as you'd ever find." He paused, frowning. "Why would this dude want to leave anything to us? Our great-grandfather disowned Grandpa Vazken for marrying outside the community."

"The community?" Charles asked.

"The Armenian community in Chicago. Grandpa married an Irish woman, Mary O'Reilly. A real sweetheart, but boy did she have a temper. My family claims she gave it to me along with her eyes."

"Oh, so that was the problem," Alex said. "I didn't realize Armenians were as tight-knit as that."

"They aren't quite as bad here in California." He leaned back in his chair once more and crossed his sandaled feet in front of him, taking a sip of latte. "I can't imagine his fortune will amount to much after it's divided among us. We've got a big family." Alex noted his interest in her appeared to be greater than any interest he might have in a legacy. Despite Charles's presence, he was examining her face and figure with the eyes of a connoisseur.

The one thing Alex hated about her job, when working for Richard, was that inheritances always brought out the worst in people who might otherwise be perfectly normal. But this man didn't seem to fit the pattern. For all the interest he showed, she might have told him he'd inherited a pigsty. *But, of course, this man could be a terrific actor.*

"Did a man named Leon Mugerian ever get in touch with any of you?" Alex asked. "He claimed to be a genealogist. He's the one who found you for Paul Mardian."

"Mugerian?" Vaz appeared to be searching his memory. *But he could be faking it.* "You'll have to ask the others, but I never talked to him or anyone claiming to be a genealogist."

"Could you give me the names of all your grandfather's descendants?"

The man drew a deep breath. Alex took her notebook and a pen from her carryall.

"My grandfather had three children: Jivan, Nancy, and Panos. My dad's Jivan. He made a pile in Orange County real estate and lives on Balboa Island. I have a brother, Thomas, who owns this espresso bar, and you met his son, Benji, who works for me when he's not surfing. My kids are preteens—Vazken III and a daughter, Caroline."

Alex scribbled all this down.

"Another latte?" Charles asked the Armenian.

"Please. What I really feel like I need is a shot of brandy."

Charles left the table, and Vaz continued. "New family: my aunt Nancy Arkesian. She was widowed young and passed away in '92 from an aneurysm. She left two children, George and Mary. George is a pompous attorney, and Mary's a nurse. *She's* a sweetie pie. Her son, Dennis, just had his tenth birthday. George doesn't have kids yet."

Writing quickly, Alex managed to get this down by the time Charles returned with Vaz's second latte. "Okay, now I'm ready for Panos."

"Well, he's an invalid. Construction contractor. Fell off a roof. He lives with his second son, John, in Laguna. John's a landscape contractor for the Irvine Company. He and Brittani have three rug rats. Panos's other son, Henry, is the family jerk. He's the only one of all of us who's a failure, so he hates the rest of us like poison."

"Wow," said Alex. "That's one big family."

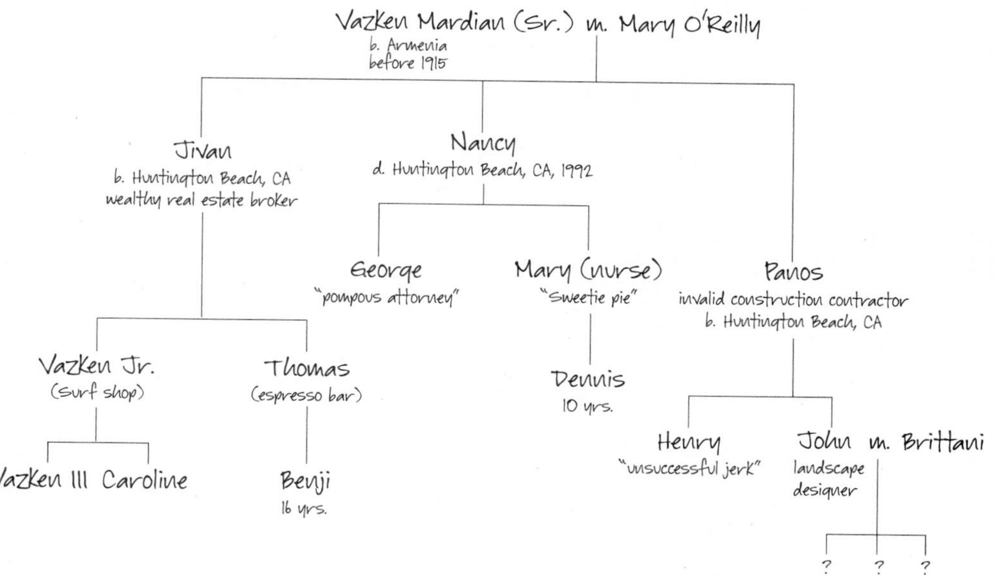

"Like I said, it's got to be a heck of an inheritance to benefit any of us very much, I suppose."

Charles intervened. "Have you any idea what a big invention the pop-top was? We're talking billions, I'm certain."

"He invented the pop-top? Geez!" Vaz looked merely shocked, not avaricious.

Alex said, "We'll need to have a meeting with the whole family present, so the estate lawyer can read the will and discuss your inheritance with you. He's back at the store, and if I'm right, he's probably been bullied into purchasing a wet suit and a boogie board."

Vaz grinned for the first time. It changed his entire face, giving him a piratical countenance.

Out of nowhere, police sirens pierced the night, coming toward them. Vaz stood and watched as they stopped in front of his store.

Pushing his chair over, he ran.

Chapter Four

Alex and Charles followed, but a police officer already had the entrance secured. Vaz was telling him that he was the owner and his nephew was in the store. The fit young officer gripped Vaz's upper arm and led him through the gathering crowd.

"What could have happened?" Alex asked Charles. "I hope Briggie and Marigny are all right."

"What about Richard?"

"I guess I should worry about him, too, but I'm too busy blaming him for getting us into this," Alex said. "He didn't need a genealogist. The Mardians were in the telephone book. He just wanted an excuse to take Briggie on vacation and propose to her while she was fishing or something."

"And Marigny?"

"Chaperone, so Briggie wouldn't object."

The crowd was thinning now, and Alex saw that a man in plain clothes was heading toward one of the bevy of patrol cars. His arm encircled Marigny as he tried to protect her from the crowd.

Galvanized by the sight of Marigny in trouble, Alex surged forward, leaving Charles behind. "Excuse me, excuse me, excuse me!"

She reached the black Crown Victoria parked behind the patrol cars at the same time as the policeman and Marigny. Tears had streaked the girl's mascara and she was still sobbing.

"Officer, I am this girl's guardian!" Alex fibbed desperately. "She's only sixteen. What are you charging her with?"

The policeman turned hard green eyes upon her. "I'm not charging her with anything. She's a witness to a kidnapping, and I'm taking her into protective custody."

Whose kidnapping? My gosh, where are Richard and Briggie?

"Then I must insist that you take me with you. She's underage. We're here from Kansas City, vacationing."

The red-headed policeman with a Marine haircut gave her a long, unflinching stare. Then he nodded shortly and motioned for her to get inside. The unmarked car smelled like cigars. Marigny followed, still sobbing. Alex gathered her into her arms, and while the officer waited for his partner to shoulder himself through the crowd, she whispered in the girl's ear. "What happened, Marigny?"

The girl took a deep breath. "That beautiful boy. The one behind the counter." Then she began crying again.

Alex thought of the "beautiful boy," Vaz's nephew, and pressed, "What happened, sweetie?" Her arm tightened around Marigny's shoulders. How could anyone kidnap someone in that crowded store and get away with it? What had Marigny seen that made her such a valuable witness? Was she in danger? Should she call Daniel?

All Marigny could do was cry. Finally, she shook her head. "He was happy to see these two guys. Real tanned. Buff. I'm sure they were surfers. I thought maybe they were friends of his. I was watching him. He has a beautiful smile."

"Did they kidnap him right in front of you?"

She shook her head again, and for another moment, she couldn't talk. "They took him into the back room. I thought it was strange for the boy to leave the cash register."

Alex guessed the next part. She knew the girl's impetuosity. "How long did you wait until you went back there?"

"Well, like, I kind of wanted to, like, meet him. So I walked up to the curtains that were hanging in front of the back room. There was, like, no sound. It was like no one was back there. So I started worrying about the cash register. There was this big line. So I, like, decided I'd better check and see what was happening."

She got no further. The sobs were shaking her whole body.

"What did you see?" Alex asked softly. At the same moment, the car began to pull out into the heavy traffic. Marine Haircut sat in the passenger seat and barked orders into his police radio.

Marigny said, "Nothing at first. There was no one there. It just felt, you know, like there was something wrong. Then I saw the note."

"What did it say, for heaven's sake?" Alex was finding it almost impossible to control her impatience.

Marigny put her head in her hands and spoke, "That these guys had been sent to kidnap Benjamin Mardian. That the person who had hired them knew his family had a lot of money and they wanted part of it. They said it was 'only fair.'"

"And you got a good look at the kidnappers?"

She nodded again.

"Was it you who called the police?"

She shuddered. "On my cell phone—Dad got me one for emergencies. I waited right there."

"Honey, why didn't you go to Briggie and your grandpa?"

"I was, like, frozen to the spot."

"Well, you did a good job, Marigny. Good job. I'm really sorry you had to see that, though. I think I'm going to call your dad. He needs to know what's going on. You could be in danger."

Marigny fished in her purse and brought out her cell phone, handing it mutely to Alex. She dialed Daniel's number from memory.

"Marigny?" he answered.

"Alex," she corrected. "Look, Daniel, Marigny's had some trouble. She's a witness in a kidnapping. I'm with her in the police car, but I think you ought to take the first flight out here. There's a possibility she might be in danger. She saw the kidnappers. I think she's the only one who can identify them."

"Criminy, Alex! I didn't know you were going with Dad. I didn't think there'd be any trouble this time. I just thought he wanted to take a jaunt with Briggie."

"I doubt this has anything to do with the case, Daniel. Marigny was just in the wrong place at the wrong time."

"Let me talk to her, please."

Alex handed the telephone to Marigny.

"Hi, Dad," was all she was able to get out when she started crying again.

The soothing tones of Daniel's voice seemed to calm her eventually. As Alex well knew, Daniel was very good in a crisis.

"I'm never going to forget it, Dad! I'm going to have nightmares 'til I die! I'm sure they're going to kill him! And he was so beautiful. So beautiful."

Eventually, she handed the phone back to Alex.

"I will fly out tonight. What are the sleeping arrangements there? Dad said he was going to the Hyatt Regency."

"Marigny has her own room, but I'll send Briggie in there, and bring her in with me. There's a king. I'll even sleep with her in case she has nightmares."

"She needs a sedative badly. Let me talk to the officer in charge."

Alex tapped the policeman in front of her on the shoulder as they rounded a corner. "Marigny's father in Kansas City would like to talk to you."

The red-headed officer took the phone. "Lieutenant Rhodes. Yes, sir. Yes. I agree, sir. We'll see to it. She's pretty shaken up." He turned to his driver. "Take a detour to the ER, Sergeant. We're going to get this little gal something to calm her down. Her dad's a doctor."

After the police expedited a quick visit to a busy emergency room that seemed miles away, Alex saw that Marigny received a shot of Ativan. Then they proceeded to the police station. The officers had been so busy coordinating forensics as well as the search for other witnesses and the kidnappers (Marigny had apparently been able to report that one of them wore a light blue windbreaker) that they hadn't taken time to introduce themselves.

"I'm Lieutenant Rhodes," the redhead said. "And this is Sergeant Switzer. I imagine the FBI will be taking over from us, since this is a kidnapping, but we need to get on it right away. Are you feeling well enough to answer some questions now?"

Marigny nodded. "If Alex can come with me."

The lieutenant looked toward Alex. "Where were you when the kidnapping took place, ma'am?" he asked.

"Down the street at the outdoor espresso bar with my fiancé and the victim's uncle."

"Well, now. That could be useful. Let's just go down to a room where we won't be interrupted."

The police station looked new and not grimy like ones she had visited in the past. Holding on to Marigny's elbow, she went with her into a beige room that had no windows, a beige table, and several beige metal chairs. They all sat down.

Lieutenant Rhodes placed a tape recorder on the table with his surprisingly well-groomed hands, and the interview began. "This is the statement of Marigny Grinnell, witness in the kidnapping of Benjamin Mardian on the evening of July 14, 1994. Miss Grinnell, could you tell us what you saw tonight in Vaz Mardian's Surfboards Unlimited?"

"Well," Marigny blushed and ran her tongue over her lips, "I was, like, watching this guy. The one who got kidnapped. Benjamin?"

The policeman nodded.

"He had a great smile and he looked like a real surfer. I was kind of . . . well, like daydreaming, when all of a sudden these guys come up to him. They didn't have anything to buy, so I thought they were just friends. Benjamin's face, like, lit up. He knew the guys, I'm sure."

"Could you describe, in as much detail as you can, what Benjamin's visitors looked like?"

Marigny described two surfers in knee-length jeans shorts and Hawaiian shirts wearing baseball caps. The windbreaker was the only difference between them. "They were both blond."

"Did you hear any sounds of an argument?"

"No. But the store was real noisy. I waited about five minutes, I think, before I went to tell . . . uh . . . Benjamin that there was a line of people waiting to buy stuff."

"So whatever happened, it was quick," Lieutenant Rhodes said.

"Yeah. I really don't think they had time to get into an argument."

"Thanks, Miss Grinnell." He noted the time the interview was concluded and then asked Alex for her name, stated it into the recorder, and began questioning her.

"What is the name of the victim's uncle, Ms. Campbell?"

"Vazken Mardian. He's the owner of the shop."

"How well do you know Vazken Mardian?"

"I just met him for the first time tonight. We had some family business to discuss."

"He's a relative?"

"No. I'm a genealogist, and I was questioning him about his family. We have been hired by his cousin's estate to identify the heirs. He's one of them."

"Ahh," Rhodes leaned back in his chair. Alex could see the thought go through his mind. *Money. Now we're getting someplace.*

"Is it a substantial estate?"

"Yes. Worth billions, probably."

Lieutenant Rhodes nodded his head and half-shut his eyes. Alex imagined his mind was racing. "And Mr. Mardian? Was he expecting this, do you think?"

"No, I would say not. He said he'd never heard of the benefactor. Vaz's grandfather quarreled with his great-grandfather. Vaz's grandfather was cut off and came to live in California where, it seems, all of his descendants now live."

"Have you been in touch with any other members of the family?"

"No, we just arrived from Kansas City this evening. Vaz Mardian had his surf shop, so we thought we'd drop in and see if we could catch him. We needed a descendancy chart of the heirs of his grandfather so we could see what we were dealing with. Of course, we had to let him know why we needed it. To say he was surprised is putting it mildly."

"Did you have time to make your chart?"

"Barely. I had just finished it when we heard your sirens."

"May I take a look?"

"It's very rough," Alex apologized, handing it to him.

Lieutenant Rhodes wrinkled his heavy brow, turning the paper this way and that to read Alex's notes. Finally, he said into the recorder, "What I have here is a chart of the descendants of Vazken Mardian, Senior, who have come into a large inheritance from their distant cousin, Paul Mardian. There are three children of Vazken—Jivan, Nancy, and Panos. These people all have children and grandchildren. A photocopy of this chart will be included with this recording."

He turned to Alex again, asking how she had known where to look for the missing cousins. She explained about the genealogist's letter attached to the will.

"So this Mugerian had visited with all these people and no one thought anything about it?"

"Mr. Vazken Mardian had never heard of him but said he might have talked to someone else in the family," Alex told him. "I don't know how Mugerian came by his information." She wondered if she should mention her theory that there was no Mugerian, just a masquerading member of the California Mardian clan. She decided not to. She hadn't had a lot of luck with policemen in the past.

There was a knock at the door. The lieutenant switched off the recorder and went to answer it. It was his partner, Switzer, whose hair was so blond it was almost invisible.

"Hammer just brought in the boy's uncle for questioning. There are also three rather insistent friends of Ms. Campbell waiting."

"I think we're finished here for now. We'll go talk to Vazken Mardian. There's a fortune involved, and I'm not at all sure this isn't tied up with it." Turning back to Alex and Marigny, he said, "We'll send Officer Hammer back to the hotel with you, as Dr. Grinnell requested. He'll keep watch outside your door. What are your plans for tomorrow?"

"We'd like to assemble the family, if possible, and read the will," Alex said.

"As I said, this will be turned over to the FBI, so I'll let them know. Do you think you can be their eyes and ears? I'm afraid their presence will keep people from reacting naturally."

"I'll do what I can," she promised.

Alex was glad Daniel was coming. She didn't want sole responsibility for anyone as unpredictable and vulnerable as Marigny. Especially when she was in danger from kidnappers.

Chapter Five

Officer Hammer turned out to be a very young cop with a crew cut and penetrating blue eyes. Had Marigny not still been in shock, Alex knew she would have tried to flirt with him. As it was, the girl was heavy with fatigue, totally unaware that her face was streaked with mascara and her ringlets straggly.

Alex greeted her anxious friends who were waiting in the lobby of the police station. "Marigny and I had to give statements. Did you see what happened, Briggs?"

Charles came up to her and planted a kiss on her forehead.Then he turned to Marigny and patted her shoulder. "Brave girl," he said. Richard took his granddaughter into his embrace and held her tightly. She began to cry again, but because of the sedative, it was more restrained.

"No," Briggie replied, "and I didn't hear anything, either. I just wondered why no one was around to let me pay for my wet suit and boogie board. Then the cops came and got Marigny. They won't tell us anything. What happened?"

"She's had a frightening experience. Let's get her back to the hotel, and then we'll talk. She's sleeping in your bed, Briggs. You'll have to take her room."

When they returned to the Hyatt Regency, Charles retrieved Marigny's things, and Richard helped Briggie take her luggage down to her new room. Alex put the girl straight to bed. She was nearly dropping with fatigue as the adrenaline left her body and the sedative took over.

Officer Hammer, who looked a little uncertain of himself, touched his automatic weapon as though to make certain it was there and then took a chair out into the hall to begin his vigil. As soon as Alex was certain Marigny was asleep, she motioned Charles, Briggie, and Richard to be seated in the sitting room of her suite. She related all that had occurred.

"Glory!" said Briggie. "Here we go again!"

"We don't really know that this has anything to do with the case, Briggs," Alex objected. "I mean the estate won't be settled for months, because it has to go through probate. According to the ransom note, these Mardians have substantial wealth of their own."

"Maybe it's the old 'eliminating the heirs' trick," Briggie said.

"We've thought that before and it's always come to nothing. Besides, according to Vaz, no one knew about this bequest."

Richard was rubbing his upper lip with his finger. Alex was reminded of Vaz's identical gesture. "We'll have to find out if all the heirs are wealthy. Maybe these thugs were hired by someone in the family."

Charles, who was sitting on the couch with his arm around Alex's shoulders, spoke for the first time. "Why don't you show them your descendancy chart, Alex?"

Pulling it out of her pocket, she handed it to Briggie. "Lots of descendants, but there's lots of money to go around," Briggie said.

"And if no one knew they were getting it, then it can't be a motive, after all."

"The police don't agree. They've hopped right on to this inheritance thing. I don't think they've even considered anything else," Alex mused.

"Well, I'm ready for bed," Briggie announced. "It's been a long day." She handed the chart back to Alex. "We'll get busy sorting out these people in the morning and telling them of their good fortune."

Richard said, "I suppose you've notified Daniel?"

"Yes, he insisted Marigny be given a sedative before she was questioned. He's on the night flight."

"Good." Richard climbed to his feet ponderously. "I think I'll turn in, too. Let's go, Brighamina."

When they were alone at last, Alex turned to Charles. "Okay, buddy, out with it. What's wrong? You've been acting strange all day."

Charles's sky blue eyes clouded, and a frown line appeared between his brows. He leaned forward, his elbows on his knees and his chin in his hands. It was a very un-Charles-like pose.

"My mother's had a heart attack, Alex. A bad one. They did surgery yesterday."

She sat up straight with a sharp vision of Charles's sweet mother in a hospital bed, deathly pale. "What in the world are you doing here? You should be in Oxford!"

He put his face in his hands. "I'd only make her worse. The thing is . . . well . . . she had it because I joined the Mormon church. She's terribly upset. She says I'm no longer a Christian, that I've joined a cult and generally put myself beyond the pale."

Alex closed her eyes. She felt as though she had been dealt a blow to the solar plexus. Though Briggie had told her there were a lot of misunderstandings about the Mormons, she had never personally encountered any. But Charles was descended from generations of

Oxonians who had turned progressively more secular. Trying to keep her voice even, she said, "I'm so sorry, Charles. When will you know the outcome of the surgery?"

"It's Hannah's fault," he said, speaking of his sister-in-law as though Alex hadn't spoken. "She's very committed to the Church of England, which is quite odd in our generation. When she heard what I'd done, she went to her priest, and he told her only lower class Brits joined the Mormon church because of the welfare program. He said that our view of Jesus Christ is heathen."

"Heathen!" she exclaimed, suddenly angry. "Geez Louise! Where would he get such an idea?"

Charles merely shrugged.

"I'm so sorry, love." She had never called Charles "love" in her life. But she knew he was hurting terribly. Even more than she was. "You must feel awful."

When he turned to her, his eyes were wild. "Have I done the right thing?"

She was stunned. This was so unlike the self-assured Charles she knew. "You think you made a mistake?"

"It seemed the right thing at the time, but now I just don't know. Hannah told me that I've as much as killed my mother. If being baptized was the right thing, why would this happen? I never dreamed anyone would be upset."

Alex retreated into herself, feeling as though her heart was wringing itself into knots. "I'm sorry," was all she could think of to say. What would she do in Charles's position, after all? Was her testimony strong enough to withstand scorn and terrible pain to her family? She knew she never would have been baptized if Stewart were alive. His reaction would have been belittling and contemptuous. And Charles's mother's heart attack? All she could think of was that the woman probably felt like she'd nurtured a snake in her bosom when she'd welcomed Alex to the family.

"Alex, what am I to do?" he asked. It hurt her further that he needed to ask this question.

"I don't know, Charles," she said tightly. "I can see where you'd be terribly upset about your mother and Hannah's prejudice, but I thought you were certain that the Church was the true church of Jesus Christ. It's not like you to be wishy-washy."

"Perhaps I'm a moral coward," he said sadly, not looking at her.

"Charles! You know you're not! Anyway, this really has nothing to do with me. It's between you and God." She studied the profile she loved so much. She couldn't be wrong about him! He was more than just a pretty face with a thick slathering of charm. He was deeply caring and full of unplumbed depths she was only beginning to see. If he weren't, he would never have taken this news about his mother so hard.

More to the point, could she possibly give him up? The first person she had trusted? Did she love him more than she loved God?

Taking a deep breath that actually hurt, she tried with every bit of her neophyte testimony to be firm. "You've got to go home. Back into your real environment. See if you really believe The Church of Jesus Christ of Latter-day Saints is God's restored church on earth. If the Book of Mormon is true. I know it's the cornerstone of your testimony. If your mother makes it through surgery, spend time with her. She needs to know she hasn't lost her son."

"But Alex, you're my life! How can I leave you?"

His plea grabbed at her heart. What woman could resist such a cry? And when she was a new convert, hadn't she needed Briggie, didn't she still need Briggie? Was her faith enough to withstand this? Was she strong enough to go on alone, leaving Charles behind for the rest of her life if he decided he couldn't proceed with his baptismal covenants? Could she give up a warm, flesh-and-blood love in exchange for the story of Joseph Smith and his gold plates?

"I won't go without you," he said, suddenly intransigent.

"You're afraid they'll sway you, aren't you?"

"You're my touchstone, Alex. I love you with all my heart. I don't want to be away from you. I don't want to lose you."

She felt as though Armageddon itself were going on inside her. "I don't want to be lost," she said quietly. "But if there's one thing I've learned, it's that humans are fallible. I'm not strong enough for both of us, Charles. I'm just learning to trust the Savior myself. It's taken me a long time to get to this point."

Charles stood and began to pace, more agitated than she'd ever seen him.

Thinking furiously, she was surprisingly calm. "I think maybe the Savior needs to be our touchstone," she said finally. "For both of us. If we're both trying to trust in Him, then that striving will bring us together, not pull us apart." Alex had no idea where this thought had sprung from. She envisioned two people swimming upstream, trying to reach a moss-covered stone as though their lives depended upon it.

"That's a lovely image," Charles said, seating himself again at her side. "But are you sure we need a specific church?"

Alex stood and walked over to the sliding glass door that led to her balcony. Opening the door, she slipped outside and leaned against the balcony rail. The ocean was not far away. She could hear its soothing rhythm, and her mind flashed back to the moment when she first knew she loved Charles. They had been punting down the Cherwell River at Oxford. He had stood above her like a god. He smiled, and for the first time since she was fourteen, when her mother had become an abusive alcoholic, the world had seemed glorious. *This is the way love is supposed to feel.* She remembered the heat of the summer sun on her back, as though it were burning away all her tragedies, telling her that this man belonged to her.

For a long time, she had resisted. He was too handsome to trust. He'd had lovers. How could he love or understand the ordinary Mormon American, Alex Campbell?

As though responding to her question, he came up behind her and began to gently kiss her neck and hair. His hands were urgent on her shoulders. Turning in his arms, she kissed him ferociously, trying to imprint her being upon his soul. *She couldn't give him up. He was marrow to her bone.*

"I'll be waiting," she promised.

"You're not going to cut and run?"

She battled back the uncertainties. "I won't say it isn't tempting. It's been my m.o. for too long. But I honestly don't want to live without you, Charles. And now I really don't know how I'd get on from day to day without the gospel. It's a conundrum. Your doubts are tearing me in two."

His face mirrored her misery. She drew his head down with her hands on either side and kissed him slowly and sweetly. "Christ will heal us, if we let Him," she whispered between kisses. "We just need faith, I think. If this is His true church, don't you think He'll help us?"

He had told her once that she and his first cousin Philippa were the only women in his life whom he was certain saw beyond his looks to the man inside. Right now, she wished she could reach inside that man and brand the gospel on his heart. Her favorite hymn came to mind:

Prone to wander, Lord, I feel it,
Prone to leave the God I love;
Here's my heart, O take and seal it;
Seal it for Thy courts above.

Alex felt tears start in her eyes and blinked them away hastily. "I love you so much, Charles."

"Oh, Alex." He held her close. "How I hope that's true."

"Good. Briggie's always told me that faith begins with hope."

Charles smoothed the lines between her brows. "My greatest hope is that there will be a future for us," he said. "That we can find a way to resolve this. I never knew how much it was possible to love someone."

After another lengthy kiss, he was gone. Alex felt as though an iron portcullis had crashed down between them at the closing of the door.

Chapter Six

Alex slept very little next to the sedated Marigny. She kept recalling Briggie's counsel to trust the Savior to pick up her burdens when they were too difficult or uncontrollable for her to bear. Surely this, of all things, was a test of that counsel.

Finally, she did a mental exercise. She walked to the edge of her known world, and before she could drop off into the hell of abandonment, she prayed, "I can't do this alone, Lord. Even Briggie can't help. I'm sending Charles back to his old, easy bachelor's life, and he only has six months of experience with the gospel. I don't know how strong he'll be against the derisiveness of his family. He needs Thee. And I need Thee to keep me from shutting down, turning away, and giving up. Please, please help!"

She felt herself step back from the edge. Sweet warmth enveloped her like a cloak. Pure love pierced her breast, and she felt a calm she had never experienced. Briggie's wisdom hadn't been a palliative. She called it the healing power of the Atonement. And, for the moment at least, it had worked. Just as when she had forgiven her mother, the

Atonement worked. Clinging to an image of the Savior praying for her soul in Gethsemane, she finally slept.

Alex and Marigny woke in the morning to an unceremonious pounding on their door.

Drat! She didn't have a bathrobe. Pulling on jeans under Charles's crew shirt, she ran a hand through her curls and went to answer.

It was Daniel, foursquare and solid but hollow-eyed with fatigue. He pulled her into a comforting hug. "Is she still asleep?"

"I think you just woke her."

Marigny came running from the bedroom, still wearing her shorts and shirt from the night before. "Dad! Oh, Dad! I've never been so glad to see you!" She embraced Daniel and began to kiss him all over his face.

"Whoa there, girl! I'm happy to see you, too. Trust you to be in the thick of things."

"But it was awful, Dad. Terrible. I'll never forget it."

"We can do some work on that, honey. Don't worry. For once I can be truly useful to you."

Alex was touched by the tenderness with which Daniel stroked his daughter's face and hair. He was such a good person and had tried so hard with Marigny. But the teenage years had been difficult for both of them without a wife and mother.

"Why don't you go shower and get dressed, Mare," he suggested. "I'm starved. I imagine they have an IHOP somewhere around here."

"IHOP! You never take me to IHOP!"

"Well, view it as a reward for being so brave."

"Can Alex come?" So Marigny was still not above a little matchmaking.

"I imagine she'll be breakfasting with Charles," Daniel said gently.

Alex intervened, "Charles has left. His mother has had a heart attack and is in critical condition. He's gone back to Oxford."

Both father and daughter brightened. Alex sighed.

"You do like IHOP, don't you, Alex?" Marigny asked.

"Love it," she said. "You go shower, and I'll bring your dad up to speed."

They sat on the shrimp-colored couch after Alex had poured Daniel some canned orange juice from the refrigerator. "Personally, I think this is nasty, but it will help your blood sugar," she said.

Then she told him in detail about the events of the night before, stopping short of the complicated descendancy chart.

"Any ideas about who would want to kidnap the boy?" Daniel asked finally.

"None. The police think it has to do with the estate your dad is administering because of the money angle, but I disagree. It doesn't make any kind of sense. You see, supposedly, no one knew about it. But, to be honest, I think one of these heirs could still be a murderer. Your dad's client was a billionaire, and he was murdered in Kansas City two weeks ago." She explained her impersonation theory regarding the supposed genealogist.

"Geez! And Dad dragged Marigny into this? I thought he just wanted her to see the ocean."

"He was a little thoughtless. For some reason, even after hanging around us for so long, he never thought the murder would have anything to do with the heirs."

"So I suppose you're going to try to solve it."

Alex grinned. "What do you think?"

Daniel groaned and ran a hand through his ginger-colored hair. "I would have thought your adventures in the Ozarks would have permanently cured you of meddling in murderous family trees."

"Think of it as my calling. You can take Marigny home. That would probably be the safest thing."

"Does anyone know that she can identify the kidnappers?"

"I think the surf shop owner may have guessed it, since the police hauled her away. But he didn't see us together, so I don't think he has any idea who she is."

Daniel appeared to consider this. "You know what? I think I'll take a little vacation. I've never been to California before. And Marigny is not going to let me drag her home. I sure can't count on Dad to look after her. He'll be too busy sparring with Briggie."

"Did you know he proposed to her?"

Daniel's jaw dropped. "Holy mackerel! Has he lost his mind?"

"You know, I've thought about it, and I think she makes him feel young and adventurous. Unless I'm wrong, they'll be body surfing in twin wet suits before the week is out." Alex grinned at Daniel's rueful expression.

"Has she accepted?"

"Heavens, no. He's not a member of our church. She says they wouldn't be compatible."

Daniel ran *both* hands through his hair. "Even without the difference in religion, their marriage would resemble an old 'I Love Lucy' scenario." He shook his head. "They'd be in trouble all the time, Alex. Are we ready for that?"

Alex didn't miss the "we." "Why don't you go have a shower yourself, while I get ready for our gourmet breakfast?" she advised.

"I have to call my office first. Got to get Betty to cancel my appointments for the week, and refer all the urgent ones to my partner."

"So you're staying?" *What a rotten time for Charles to take off!*

"You couldn't drag me away from the spectacle of my father

courting Briggie. And I'm not easy about Marigny. She'd pout for a month if I took her home, though."

While Marigny was still monopolizing the bathroom, Alex called her colleague.

"My stars, Alex, I was still asleep. Can you believe it? It must be true what they say about the sea air."

"Daniel has shown up to take Marigny and me out to breakfast. He's planning on helping us trap this murderer."

Briggie laughed. "Déjà vu."

"Yeah."

"How does Charles feel about your going out to breakfast with your old beau?" Though she had always tried to be impartial, Briggie had clearly favored Daniel's suit for her hand. At least until Charles had joined the Church.

All of Alex's ideas about the case, which she had been forcing herself to concentrate on, flew out the window and into the Pacific. "Oh, Briggie, I've got to talk to you. Can you hang around after breakfast? Something really, really awful has happened."

"Glory, Alex! You expect me to wait until then to find out? You come over to my room this instant."

Alex wanted nothing more than to do exactly as Briggie said. What had she been thinking of to contemplate breakfast with Daniel and Marigny?

As soon as the girl was out of the shower, she said, "Marigny, tell your dad I had to meet with Briggie about the case, will you? Benji's kidnapping put it out of our minds, but Briggie has hardly even seen the descendancy chart."

Daniel's daughter looked like she was going to sulk, but then a thought arrested her. Probably the realization that her father had a clear field, now that Charles was gone.

Charles. Gone. Alex said, "I've got to have a shower. Apologize to your father, will you? Thanks, Marigny. Have fun!"

Her tears mingled with the shower spray. What was wrong with her? She had put it in the Lord's hands. She ought to be serene and faithful after last night's extraordinary experience. But life hadn't prepared her to be full of faith regarding the future, and just at the moment, she was finding it hard. This was going to be a battle, not an easy win. The fact was, Charles had his agency. Once he was back at Oxford, she wasn't going to seem very real to him. His perspective might do a kaleidoscopy thing and wheel back to the days before he had even heard of the gospel. Especially if his conversion was putting his mother's life in danger. Charles's agony at leaving was because he had sensed that something like that might happen.

She tried hard to recapture the peace she had felt after her prayer. *Leave it up to the Lord. Don't think about losing Charles. Don't even* think *it.*

The fact was, she might never see him again. Might never touch his face, be ignited by his kisses, or feel his smile on her face like sunshine.

She slammed the shower handle off. No! How absolutely soppy she was getting! She wasn't going to let any of that happen. She was through being poor pathetic little Alex. Charles loved her! If she had to, she would fly across the Atlantic and bring him home. He was changed. She knew he was! That's why she hadn't cried last night. She had to trust him. And trust the Lord. The gospel was true. Without it, his old world would make no sense to him. It would seem shallow. *But what was he going to do about his family?*

Drying herself vigorously, she told herself that it was hours before she could expect to hear from him. She had a job to do and a murder to solve. She needed to get to work.

She dressed in black slacks with a black and white striped top.

Her hair was wild in the ocean air, so she subdued it with a bright pink scrunchy on the back of her head. No time for makeup. Grabbing the descendancy chart, she made for Briggie's room.

Her friend was dressed today in royal blue polyester pants with a white Royals T-shirt. "Good," she said, studying Alex's face. "Whatever it is, you're not wallowing in it."

Briggie's words made her realize that ever since she'd known her mentor, she'd been beset by some sort of misery. But she was better now. Stronger.

"Let's sit on the balcony," she suggested. "Is Richard still sleeping?"

"We're meeting for breakfast in an hour downstairs. I expect you to join us, Alex. I'm not in the mood for any cozy little chats with his majesty."

The thought of her friend having a "cozy chat" with Richard over eggs Benedict made Alex laugh. She followed her friend outside and sat on the aqua lounge chair.

"So what gives?" Briggie asked.

"It's Charles's family, Briggs. When she heard Charles was baptized, his mother had a severe heart attack. We don't know yet if she'll recover. She had surgery yesterday. Charles has gone back to Oxford."

"Well, my stars. That sweet old lady! When we were there, she was always very nice to me, and she knew I was a Mormon!"

"Did she?"

"Yes. I had to explain why I wouldn't take tea or coffee."

"Well, it seems that Hannah—you remember Charles's brother Frederick's wife—has got hold of all the garbage about us being a cult and not being Christians. They more or less made him feel that he was no longer welcome in the family. And I sure as heck won't be!"

"How did Charles take it?"

"He was really mixed up, Briggie. Not sure of himself at all. He didn't want to leave me. I made him go. He will never forgive himself if his mother dies because of his decision."

Briggie didn't say anything for a few moments. "My Ned's family cut him off when he went from RLDS to LDS. It wasn't easy, I can tell you. Especially when the kids came along."

"I didn't know that. And they lived right there near you. That must have been really hard."

"Well, Ned just told them that they were victims of years of bitterness and slander against Brigham Young. He said if they were real Christians, they would never cut him off, and they would be real grandparents to our children. He told them they were scared."

"Hmm. I'd never thought of that. Why would Charles's mother and sister-in-law be scared?"

"Having a Mormon in the family might mean they'd be outcasts in their cozy little society. Have you ever thought about why the gospel was restored in America, Alex?"

She remembered her thoughts in Oxford—a citadel of learning since the 1500s. "Maybe because it wouldn't have been possible in the midst of all those hundreds of years of traditions in Europe."

"Right. The people who broke with the Old Country were different from the ones who stayed. The American character is different from the British character. Charles has really taken to the American way of life far more than I could have predicted."

"Well, he is part American, you know. From our great-great-grandfather."

"I wouldn't have expected you to be so serene over this, kiddo."

"I'm not really. I blubbered in the shower this morning. But I'm trying to have faith that the gospel's true, and that if Charles puts it to the test, he will see that. I know he loves me. I know he is afraid of what will happen to him when he's faced with a hostile family. And he feels guilty for his mom's heart attack. But this is an important test for him. And for me." She leaned forward so she could look directly into Briggie's beloved seamed face. "I've got to find out if I love Charles more than God. And I'm not going to be passive. If Charles decides to choose his family over me and the gospel, I'm not going to let him go without a fight. I'm going over there, Briggs. I'm going to remind him of all that we have. Right there in his own backyard."

"Good for you! That's my girl!" Briggie beamed, and Alex basked for a moment in her approval.

"Now, we've got to get down to work," she said. "As you know, Charles and I met Vâzken Mardian last night and went down to the local hangout, which happens to be owned by his brother, Thomas. Benji's dad."

Alex brought Briggie up to date, explaining the elaborate but almost illegible descendancy chart.

"Good grief! That's a lot to take in."

"Yeah. Do you think you can get Richard to try to organize a family meeting for this evening or whenever it will work? He has to read the will, preferably in one of their homes. I really think this group sounds like it holds promise, don't you?"

"Well, apparently there's scads of money around, so I think whoever went after those artifacts was in it for love, not money. Armenians are very passionate. Those antiquities could have been a real draw if we could just find out how they knew about them." Then she added, "Just in case Benji's kidnapping is related, Marigny needs to get a look at the family without them seeing her. I'll tell Richard to let us know the meeting place, and we can scope it out. Maybe Marigny could peek in a window or something."

"Very Agatha Christie, Briggs. If I didn't know better, I'd swear you were related. Daniel will insist on spying with her, I'm sure." The thought made her grin. It was like old times. Then she sobered. This was kidnapping they were talking about. "I hope this doesn't turn into a comedy or even a tragedy. It has the makings of both." She stood up. "I'm ready for breakfast, and I think it's about time. Shall we go meet your swain?"

"Well, Brighamina," Richard said after a substantial breakfast of omelets, hash browns, sausage, and fresh-squeezed orange juice, during which he had been studying the descendancy chart. "I guess we'd better go upstairs and have a go at arranging some kind of meeting. Let's start with the eldest brother, Jivan. As head of the family, maybe he'll call everyone else."

"Do you know much about the Armenian Holocaust, Richard?" Alex asked. "I think it would be good background for us to have."

"I must admit that Paul made me curious. He was so passionate about it. The seeds of it actually went back several hundred years. The Armenians were part of the Ottoman Empire, but they were always a minority because they were Christians. They were persecuted on and off by the Muslims for a long time because of it. Then the First World War came, and the Armenians sided with the Russians against the Turks. That gave them an excuse for wholesale slaughter. They began with the intellectuals in 1915. Throughout the rest of the war, they committed rape and genocide, trying to exterminate every last Armenian. They did a good job. But many of them fled."

"Thanks," Alex said. "That's really helpful."

"Well," said Briggie, "Let's go upstairs and get to work."

Jivan turned out to be dismissive at first. Richard reported, "I think he thought it was some sort of scam, all that money. He is more concerned about his grandson's kidnapping, as you can imagine. So I told him I was in the store when it happened. That broke the ice." The lawyer sat back in the large comfortable chair in his suite. "I thought it politic to tell him what a fine young man Benjamin was. Then I told him that Alex was with Vaz Jr., down the street working on the descendancy when it happened. That gave you credibility which rubbed off on me."

"Did you tell him about Paul's murder?" Briggie asked.

"No. I thought he'd had enough for one day."

"You're right. Let's do a little observation first. I assume that Jivan is going to make the rest of the calls, so you don't have to go through that again?" Alex asked.

"Yes, thank heaven. He said he'd have the clan there at his house on Balboa Island at eight o'clock. He gave me directions."

"Good work, Richard," Briggie congratulated him. "Now we can drive there and scope it out so we can see if there's any place Marigny and Daniel can get a view of the family without being seen."

Richard seemed relieved. "Anything that keeps you from insisting that I buy a wet suit and accompany you into the surf!"

Chapter Seven

There was a knock at the door. Daniel and Marigny had returned from the IHOP and a little swimsuit shopping.

"Are we ready to hit the beach?" he asked.

"We're going to do a little sightseeing first," his father told him. "My reading of the will is going to take place tonight at the kidnapped boy's grandfather's house on Balboa Island, Marigny. We need to scout it out, to see if there's a place where you can look into the house unobserved and see if you can identify anyone that looks like Benji's kidnapper."

"But it said in the note that they were acting for someone else!" the girl protested.

"I thought of that, too. But kidnappers aren't an honest bunch, and we can't afford to overlook the family itself," Briggie said.

"It sounds just like the kind of harebrained scheme you and Dad would think of," Daniel objected. "What if she's caught?"

"You'll be there to make sure she stays undercover," Alex soothed him.

Later, when they boarded Richard's rental van, Daniel cornered her in the backseat. He put his arm casually across the back. She felt uncomfortable but coolly ignored it.

Balboa Island turned out to be just the kind of place Alex would have loved when she was a teenager. As they crossed the bridge from the mainland, they crawled down the main street behind a long stream of cars. Alex saw a store that sold chocolate-covered frozen bananas, and almost demanded that Richard stop, but there was no room to park. There were fancy Italian and French bistros, expensive beachwear boutiques, and health food stores. Beautiful people with gorgeous tans, dressed in bathing suits, sundresses, or shorts, crammed the sidewalks. Marigny was in ecstasy.

"Parking is going to be a problem," the more practical Briggie said.

"Jivan told me it might be," Richard told her. "Also, it's all one-way streets. His place is right on the water, so we can park anywhere and walk to it. There's a walkway that goes all around the island."

"Briggs, this is much more fun than the Ozarks," Alex said.

"This place is way cool." Marigny peered out the window, her eyes moving rapidly in an effort to see everything. "I think I want to move here, Dad. Are there any colleges around?"

"The University of California–Irvine is right up the road," Richard told her. "It's a good school if you don't mind having an anteater as a mascot." They had turned off the main street now and were cruising through a neighborhood that consisted of houses of every size and description—some luxurious, some plain little beach cottages.

"An anteater?" Marigny said. "That's weird."

"Yeah," agreed Briggie. "Oh, Richard, I see a parking place where that van is pulling out! Hurry and get it! Put on your blinker!"

"I see it, Brighamina. Just leave it to me."

As they scrambled out of the van, Daniel helped Alex solicitously down to the street. It didn't annoy her when Charles did the same thing, but it seemed that everything Daniel did annoyed her. Why was that?

Alex looked up and down the street. Charles would have loved to see this little slice of Americana. There was a Victorian horror built on a sixteenth of an acre. Next to it was a sweet little white cottage with a red door and pottery ducks that pranced down a postage stamp-sized lawn surrounded by a white picket fence. She was willing to bet that Jivan's house would be spectacular.

"He said he lived on the west side of the island," Richard said. "Right near the ferry that goes across to the peninsula, which means we walk north once we get to the bay."

Daniel, Marigny, and Briggie were looking around in wonder as they walked toward the bay. "I don't think I'd like to be quite so close to my neighbors," Briggie remarked.

"But they'd be such fun neighbors!" Marigny told her. "This is an awesome place! I wouldn't change one thing!"

When they reached the sidewalk that encircled the island, they turned north, and Alex looked with amazement at the homes that lined Balboa Bay. They all had enormous windows looking out on the sailboats and yachts moored off the narrow strip of sand that was covered with sunbathers.

"Look at that yacht!" Daniel exclaimed. "The hull is hardwood. It's gorgeous!"

Alex was reminded of Daniel's penchant for vintage vehicles. He restored cars from the fifties, saying that it helped him relax.

After they had been walking about twenty minutes, Alex saw the ferry ahead. Richard consulted his directions. "Here we are." He pointed to a large house built of unpainted redwood that jutted out into its miniscule yard, pointed, like the prow of a ship. The front was all glass.

"Wow!" Alex said.

"Awe*some!*" Marigny echoed.

"Glory!" Briggie added.

But Daniel was worried. "It's wide open. There's no place to hide."

Alex inspected the layout. It was hard to see through the tinted glass. "Well, if I were Jivan," she said, "that would have to be my living room. By eight it will be dark enough for lights indoors. Unless he's got blinds, all you will have to do is walk by several times, slowly, and look inside, like any tourist."

Marigny giggled. "Maybe I should buy some wigs."

"Marigny!" Daniel said, obviously exasperated. "Remember yesterday? Remember Benji? This is serious business."

"Oh, that reminds me." Alex was rooting through her carryall. "If I can find my tape recorder . . . ah, here it is! I think I'm going to tape this for the FBI. They're taking over the case from the locals and will probably want to know what goes on tonight."

"Do you always carry a tape recorder around?" Daniel asked.

"Yes, as a matter of fact. I have one that I use for interviews with our clients. I can stick it in my carryall and turn it on as soon as we get there." She turned to Richard, who had somehow become their leader. "I want to ride on the ferry."

They spent the afternoon riding the ferry to the peninsula, walking down the peninsula pier admiring the surfers, and having a late lunch at a colorful Mexican restaurant. Alex ate the best chili rellenos she had ever had. But the group seemed sadly incomplete to Alex, who knew she was lacking in sparkle. And Daniel was acting proprietary, which had always irritated her.

"Missing your man, honey?" Briggie asked softly as they took the noisy ferry back to Balboa Island.

"He would love all this. But I'm anxious. Briggie, what if he got home and his mother had died?"

"Let's not invent troubles. They can do so much for heart patients these days."

"But we're talking about the British health system! Charles is full of horror stories about it."

"I bet you a sundae we'll have a nice, positive message waiting for us when we get back to the hotel."

But when they finally returned, there was no message. Alex assumed this could only mean one thing. Charles had found his mother dead and was overwhelmed with guilt and remorse. He didn't want to talk to her.

Briggie was her usual bracing self. "Buck up, Alex," she said as they stood outside the door to her suite. "You're mind reading. You always do it. Now, just concentrate on this case."

"There's nothing to concentrate on. We've done all the work. We have the descendants Richard needs."

"And one of them probably killed Paul Mardian. Do you want to see him get his inheritance? For that matter, aren't you the least bit curious about meeting these people? They sound interesting."

"Rich, you mean. And no, I'm not interested in anything but a good night's sleep. And Daniel's crowding me."

"You're whining, Alex."

Opening her door without another word, Alex went into her suite and shut the door on Briggie. Then she went to the glass door to the balcony, opened it, and stepped out into the late afternoon air. Just here they had said good-bye twenty-four hours ago. It sure had been easier on her heart before she learned to feel things again. Lying on the chaise lounge, Alex deliberately closed her eyes and let the waves lull her to sleep.

Marigny awakened her out of a lovely dream of Charles, a sunset, and a beach. "Alex, Dad said it's time to go down to dinner."

"I'm still full from lunch," she told the girl with a yawn. "You go down. I'm going to have a shower."

It was just as she was emerging from the shower that the telephone rang.

"Alex?" It was Charles. He had not been lost in the Bermuda Triangle of her fears, after all.

"Oh, Charles, tell me. How is your mother?"

"Well, she didn't die during surgery. But there was so much damage to her heart that she's critical. I can't help but wish she were in the States."

"Was she happy to see you?"

"I haven't seen her yet. I'm afraid of causing another relapse."

"Love, she wants to see you. She wants to know she hasn't lost you to some weird American religion."

"Well, it's too late tonight. It's two A.M. or something ghastly like that. I'm still on California time, and I'm missing you desperately. But I promise, I'll go in the morning."

"I'm just glad she's recovering. I've been imagining the worst, of course."

"She's tough, Alex. Remember, she came through the Blitz."

"Have you seen Frederick and Hannah?"

She heard him sigh. "Yes. I told them I never would have taken them for bigots. It's so odd, because tolerance has always been their ruling virtue."

"And how did they respond?"

"They were dumbfounded. They looked at me strangely and then changed the subject. We discussed the work I've been doing on the estate. Of course, they're anxious to know when they'll get their money."

Alex realized she had been holding her breath. Letting it out slowly, she sat down. "Well, that wasn't too bad, then."

"No. But it feels very odd being here. I feel almost like a tourist or something. It's gorgeous in the way that only Oxford can be in high summer. I didn't realize how much I'd missed it. Frederick and I have an early tennis date tomorrow."

Though she herself thought Oxford was heaven on earth, his words gave her heart a nasty jolt. But, after all, the poor man had been living in Chicago, which, in spite of its many attractions, was everything Oxford wasn't. "Then you promise me that you will go see your mother?"

"Yes, I promise."

"And you'll call me with a report?"

"Yes, darling. Has my rival for your affections arrived?"

"Unfortunately. He's treating me like cut glass, as usual. I'm so glad you know I've got a brain in my head."

"He's going to try to turn you against me."

"Probably." She decided a little uncertainty was appropriate for a man as good-looking as Charles.

"He knows things about you I'll never know, you told me."

"That's only fair. Think of the forty-six years of your bachelorhood that I know nothing about. Don't you think that bothers me?"

"Ah, but I was washed clean at my baptism."

"So, you really believe that?"

"It's the only hope this old reprobate has."

It wasn't lost on Alex that he'd turned the question into a joke. Or did he mean it? She changed the subject, telling him about their day and what was going to happen a while later.

"You know, darling, while I was there I was rather enjoying playing detective, but now it suddenly occurs to me that you might get coshed on the head again. It always seems to happen when you turn investigator."

She sighed, "Don't go sounding like Dr. Grinnell."

"Have you always been this ornery?"

"Listen to you! Talking about me like a cowboy talking about a steer!"

"You know I love you, Alex," he said, suddenly sobered. "I'll just have to pray that nothing comes between us. Please be careful."

Dropping the banter, she said, "I'm praying the same."

Chapter Eight

Alex looked at her reflection. She had chosen to go for a feminine look. Something about her interview with Vaz had given her the idea that Armenians preferred their women to be feminine. Maybe it was all in her head, but he had seemed a bit chauvinistic toward her—a little on the Old World side, despite his surfer image. She had chosen a pleated aqua gauze skirt and a white T-shirt top with a boat neck and three-quarter-length sleeves. Completing the ensemble were white sandals and a pendant with a single silver circle. She brushed out her hair with stern strokes. Then, leaving a few curly wisps around her face, she pulled the top half of her hair into a knot at the back of her head and left the rest long. This had the effect of emphasizing her high cheekbones and long neck.

Marigny looked at her and whistled. "Alex, all you need is some of my lip gloss, and you could pass for a movie star! Are you trying to impress everyone?"

She accepted the lip gloss and smiled. "It can't hurt," she said. The teenager was dressed all in black and resembled a short cat burglar. "You're dressed for your part, I see."

"Yeah. I don't want them to see me, that's for sure. I've still got to put my hair in a bun. It's so scraggly. Can you help?"

Performing this motherly task for Marigny (which she was certain the girl had manufactured) made her wonder what it would be like to have a daughter. If she and Stewart had started a family right after their marriage, she might very well have a daughter Marigny's age. And if Megan had lived . . . But now was certainly not the time to spend regrets on that.

The Jivan Mardian home was spectacular inside as well as outside. Alex reached into her carryall and turned on the miniature tape recorder. A very tanned, very handsome man who reminded Alex of Laurence Olivier opened the door and introduced himself as George Arkesian, Jivan's nephew. He looked Alex up and down in silent appraisal.

Into her mind flashed Charles's assessment of her likeness to Jeanne Moreau, the French actress, whose most famous role had been Mata Hari. She smiled, liking herself in the role of spy. This smooth man in his yellow cashmere sweater and white slacks looked as though he enjoyed money. She racked her brain but couldn't come up with his profession.

"You're Nancy Mardian's son, am I right?"

"Good for you! Brains as well as beauty. And your name is?"

"Sorry." She stuck out her hand. "Alex Campbell. And this is my business partner, Brighamina Poulson, and the estate attorney for your cousin Paul, Richard Grinnell."

"Always nice to meet a fellow member of the bar. I'm an estate lawyer myself." George shook hands with Richard and then Briggie. "Come in. Uncle is pretty upset about Benji, so I'm afraid he's not feeling very sociable."

The marble wall of the entryway was two stories high with a thin sheet of water cascading down it into a bed of rounded pebbles. The lights were recessed, and an enormous potted palm sat at the top of a short set of steps that led down to the sunken living room. There, sitting in an enormous black leather recliner, was a man who reminded Alex of a big daddy longlegs spider. He had a drink in his hand and was staring blankly out the window, but Alex had the feeling he wasn't seeing the view.

"Uncle Jivan, here are the people about your cousin's estate."

The man turned sunken dark eyes toward them. "Money. I always thought money could do anything. Now it's turned against me." His voice was a deep bass and sounded slurred. Alex noted his large nose, curiously flattened at the end. He wasn't what you'd call handsome, but virility emanated from him, even in his sorrow.

A striking redhead with very long legs rose from the gray tweed sectional and went to the man who had spoken. The chocolate Lab curled at Jivan's feet raised his head, suddenly alert. "Now, darling," she soothed, stroking the man's thick, wavy, graying hair. She had trophy wife written all over her, Alex thought. "Think of all the good we can do. We can donate it to Opera Pacific. They'll put your name on the wall of the Performing Arts Center—carved right into the marble."

"So you can swan around and look down your nose at everyone? No, thanks. I'm going to buy a bigger yacht and call it the *Benji.* Benji loves the ocean. When we get him back, he'll help me choose it." Jivan ducked away from her stroking hands to pet his dog. "This is Godiva," he told the newcomers. "I'm Jivan, and this is Janet, my . . . er . . . wife. Who are you, and what do you want?"

Turning toward her guests, the woman said, "I'm sorry, folks. What must you think of us? Jivan is terribly, terribly upset about Benji, his favorite grandson, who was kidnapped last night."

Richard responded by switching on his charm. "We're so sorry to intrude at such a painful time. I'm Richard Grinnell. I represent the Paul Mardian estate. These are my consultants, Alexandra Campbell and Brighamina Poulson. We've come to read the will."

"Yes, well, why don't you have a seat?" Janet offered. Jivan had gone back to stroking his dog while gazing out the window. "I'm certain the others will be here shortly. In the meantime, can I get anyone a drink?"

Alex darted a glance at Briggie, who was dressed in her all-purpose navy blue polyester suit and didn't look the least like a consultant, but more like a little old lady than usual. She was taking in her surroundings, and her face reflected her awe. There was another wall of cascading water on the south end of the room that was over two stories in height. Out of the wall a bronze relief of Neptune protruded, brandishing his trident. The other two walls were solid glass, providing an extraordinary view of the bay at twilight, with many of the yachts alight and the distant shore of the peninsula lit like a fairground. The North Shore had been a ritzy place for Alex to grow up, but she'd never seen anything like this house.

"Do you have orange juice?" Briggie asked gruffly.

"Why, yes, of course," Janet replied. "And you, sir?"

Alex could see the indecision on Richard's face. "I'd better keep my mind clear. Orange juice for me, too, please."

"Me, as well," Alex said. Even though she had had enough orange juice that day to float way.

Without being asked, Laurence-Olivier George ordered a scotch, neat.

"Perhaps you can take care of the drinks, George," Janet replied.

"With pleasure, Janet darling." He made no effort to hide his sarcasm.

The next arrival was a tall, very skinny man with nervous

mannerisms and thinning hair. He had clearly not inherited the Mardian charm, whoever he was.

"Dad won't be coming," he said to Janet, who had opened the door to him. "He's having one of his bad days. As soon as John can get him settled, he and Brittani will be here, though."

"Well, I'm sorry about Uncle Panos, but come in, Henry, and meet our guests."

As they were introduced, Henry shook hands with each of them briefly. Alex noted that his hands were bony but sweaty, as though he were under some kind of strain. Was he just nervous in front of strangers, or was this the killer? How would they ever know?

Until now, the mystery had been kind of a game with her to divert her from her concerns over Charles. But now, she realized what a truly daunting task it was going to be. She hoped Marigny and Daniel would have some luck recognizing Benji's kidnappers, although none of these people resembled surfers.

"I hope your father is all right," she said to the nervous man, who looked as though he were prematurely aging.

"Oh," Henry swatted the air as though shooing a fly. "He's no better or worse. He had a fall from a roof on a project he was contracting a couple of years ago. Broke his back. Then arthritis set in. He's in a wheelchair now and lives with my brother, John, in Laguna Beach."

"Glory!" said Briggie. "What an awful thing for a man who must have led such an active life!"

"Yes, well, he's tough. It's an Armenian trait, you'll find. Bred into us as survivors of centuries of persecution."

Alex raised her eyebrows and looked at her colleague. Touchy, touchy. It sounded like Henry might have a chip on his shoulder.

"Henry, what do you do for a living?" she asked, remembering belatedly that this was the man Vaz had described as a "jerk."

"I'm a professor of Middle Eastern Studies. Unlike any of my uncles or cousins, I actually *speak* and *read* Armenian, as well as Hebrew and Farsi."

"That must be an accomplishment, these days," Alex said. "Where do you teach? UC Irvine?"

"Golden State," he said, his voice clipped. He turned abruptly and walked over to the bar that was concealed nicely behind the wall with the waterfall.

George laughed. "Golden State *Community* College. I keep telling my cousin that he needs to assimilate. No one cares about the Armenian Holocaust these days. He's third generation, for Pete's sake. It's not as though he wasn't raised with the proverbial silver spoon in his mouth! His father even augments his income."

"And that is relevant because . . . ?" Henry's voice was high and tight.

His cousin just laughed again.

"Thomas isn't coming either, of course," said Janet. "Benji's father. He's pretty upset, and his wife is totally distraught. They're just waiting for the ransom demand."

Then, before the argument could resume, two beautiful people walked in the door. The man was tanned and wore cream-colored shorts, leather sandals, and a brown polo shirt open at the neck, where Alex could see the gleam of something gold. His hair was brown with golden sun streaks, and his eyes were very blue. *Ah, these must be John and Brittani.* George moved forward to greet his cousin, shaking his hand and giving his wife a peck on the cheek. Her blonde hair and pale skin identified her as being of northern European descent. She had the smooth, finished look of a professional model.

"John and Brittani, these are the people representing this strange estate. Alex, Richard Grinnell, and . . ."

"Just call me Briggie," Alex's friend said with a grin. "Everyone but Richard does."

"Nice to meet you," John replied. Brittani smiled her welcome, showing perfect teeth.

The two moved into the room, waived the offer of a drink from George, and sat down together in an enormous chair that resembled a padded clamshell. They held hands. She couldn't imagine either of them committing murder for artifacts or kidnapping Benji for ransom. They looked like money in a classy, almost North Shore way.

"Well," Richard said, "are we missing anyone who was planning to come?"

"My sister, Mary, had to work. She's a nurse," George told them. "And Vaz isn't here yet."

"Well, we'll make a little house call to her and to John's father," Richard said. "We must speak to Thomas as well. I presume that any children are underage?"

Again, the helpful George replied, "Vaz has two—both preteens. My nephew is only ten, and John and Brittani's kids are ten and under."

The throttle of a boat could be heard through the glass. Alex looked outside as a speedboat pulled up to the Mardians' pier, and Vaz leapt out and tied it off. She was struck once more by his piratical looks, though she could scarcely see him in the twilight. How appropriate that he should come by water. He breezed through the door moments later. "George, I want a gin and tonic, on the rocks. Hello, Alex! Nice to see you again. Where's your handsome sidekick?"

"Returned to England," she said. "This is my business partner, Briggie, and this is the attorney for the estate, Richard Grinnell."

"Hmm. All the better." After looking Alex over appreciatively, Vaz advanced down the stairs holding out his hand to Briggie and Richard in turn. "I'm Vaz. Hi, Dad." Kneeling by the recliner, he actually hugged his father. "Are you feeling any better?"

"Not so you'd notice. In this parody of the happy Armenians, I am definitely the odd man out. Janet has already planned how to spend the inheritance."

Vaz looked over at Janet, his eyes hard. The woman merely shrugged.

Briggie gazed at the newcomer, starry-eyed, just as Alex had feared. "You have a great boat!" Briggie said. "Do you give rides to your friends?"

Smiling at Briggie, he winked. "Sure. We can arrange something, Briggie."

"I assume we can now proceed?" Richard said in his pompous lawyer's voice.

Jivan answered, "Let's get this over with so all these people can get out of here."

With great presence, Richard opened his briefcase, reached in, and pulled out the yellow legal papers that constituted Paul Mardian's last will and testament.

Briggie rolled her eyes at Alex as the lawyer read all the preliminaries. Finally, he got to what Briggie called "the good stuff."

"'Having recently become aware of another son of Ayk Abaven Mardian called Vazken Mardian, and having no progeny of my own, I will my estate to my uncle Vazken's descendants. An exception to this bequest is my collection of Armenian antiquities, which are to be given to the Armenian Apostolic Church of Huntington Beach, where a special wing is to be built to house them. Arrangements have already been made for this project to begin immediately.'"

The room was silent for a moment. Then Janet spoke up. "There are a lot of descendants, Mr. Grinnell. Have you any idea how much they will inherit?"

"I know that the current value of the estate is five billion dollars. I will need to prove relationship of each person who alleges to be descended from Vazken Mardian before I can tell you the exact figure, and there will be a lot of taxes, but it will be considerable. The children's money will be held in trust, of course."

The room exploded in chatter. "Five billion dollars!" "Why would he leave everything to people he'd never met?" "Is this a joke?" And then, from Jivan, "Just what this family needs—more money."

"Well, Uncle," said Henry, "you may not need it, but it will certainly be helpful to me. I can retire from teaching and spend the rest of my life doing research. The area of Armenian studies is vastly neglected. And just what are these antiquities? I'm an expert. A docent for a small Armenian exhibit in Los Angeles."

Richard said, "That is problematic. I've never seen them, and they have been stolen."

Again, the group burst into chatter. Richard held up a hand. "You might be interested to know that your generous cousin lost his life in his encounter with the burglar."

This silenced everyone, and they looked at Richard.

"To put it in plain language, Paul Mardian was murdered," Briggie said flatly.

"If any of you are interested in details, I have made photocopies of the newspaper article reporting the crime," Richard told them.

Only Professor Henry Mardian came forward. "This is disgraceful!" he said. "It says here the collection was worth millions! What would a thief do with it?"

"Maybe he's one of those people who like to gloat over their private collections," Alex said. In her opinion, Henry Mardian fit the profile of someone who might do that. His identification with his past seemed almost pathological.

"My sympathy goes out to the poor man," Brittani said. "He was a good man, making such an effort to find us, and to leave us all that money! Not that we really need it, though."

"Actually," Richard said, "he was dying of pancreatic cancer, which is why he went to such lengths to find you. He was very generous to his community, but he wanted to leave his fortune to his kin. If he hadn't been murdered, I'm sure he would have made the effort to come out to meet you."

John spoke up. "I agree with Britt. Maybe one of us should do some work researching his life and commission a bust of him to go in the Armenian church where he wanted to leave his treasures. Vaz told me he invented the pop-top can. It sounds to me like he was ingenious and deserves to be remembered."

Jivan waved his hand. "I can't think about it now. Maybe when Benji comes back . . ."

Vaz said, "Of course, Dad. All this is kind of hard to take in on top of the kidnapping. But we're going to get Benji back. The FBI is on the case now. They spoke to me this afternoon."

George had no comment, Alex noticed. He just sat looking like the cat who ate the canary.

Chapter Nine

Alex, would you like a ride back to Huntington Beach in my boat?" Vaz asked her after all the hubbub had died down and everyone had been told what kind of documentation Richard needed.

Knowing he couldn't possibly have kidnapped Benji, since she was his alibi, and feeling that he was affected least by his inheritance, Alex decided not to pass up the opportunity to find out more about the family. "That'd be great. I grew up on Lake Michigan. I love boats."

Leaving a disgruntled Briggie and Richard, she followed Vaz to the door, saying to everyone, "Nice to meet all of you. I'm sure we'll be seeing you again."

The evening air was chilly, and she rubbed her arms. That was certainly a change from the Midwest. Here, it seemed, as soon as the sun set, the ocean breezes picked up and cooled everything down.

"She's a sweet thing," she told Vaz, referring to his speedboat. His hair blew in the breeze, and it didn't seem to bother him at all that he wore only shorts and a T-shirt. "What do you call her?"

"The *Caroline.*"

"Wife?" Alex asked.

"Daughter. I don't have a wife."

Alex wondered if the mother of Caroline was dead or divorced. Vaz helped her carefully into the boat and then cast off. In a moment they were on their way, puttering south through Balboa Bay so they could round the head of the peninsula. "That will must have come as a surprise," she said. "Not that any of you seem hard up or anything."

He grinned at her, his long hand on the throttle, and to her disgust, she found him attractive. *Good grief! What's wrong with me? Since Charles got rid of my walls, am I going to be attracted to every handsome man I meet?*

"Well, money always comes in handy. Since you and Charles told me about it, I've been thinking I may pick up the lease on some property that just became available on the waterfront and expand my store." He smiled again, his teeth white in the growing darkness. "So what's the situation between you and the Englishman?"

Alex sighed and shrugged. "Complicated."

"You're wearing an engagement rock."

"We're having kind of a trial separation."

"Before you're even married? That doesn't sound hopeful."

"I'd walk on nails for Charles, so don't get the wrong idea," Alex said.

They moved out into open water, and Vaz gave the engine full throttle, making talk impossible. The spray of water on her face and in her hair invigorated her, chilly though it was.

Rounding the peninsula, the *Caroline* jetted through the ocean at top speed. Vaz turned his face away from her and concentrated on maneuvering the boat back and forth through the water, as though he were weaving a pattern. Alex took the scrunchy out of her hair and let it blow loose in the salty, wet wind. How Briggie would love this!

It took only about twenty minutes before they pulled into the slip where Vaz kept his boat. Helping her out, he said, "I've got my car parked over there." He indicated a nearly deserted parking lot. "Let me just tie her off here."

They walked up to a BMW convertible coupe. She should have known Vaz would have the best of everything. "Let's go drop in on my brother, Thomas. We can give him the news, and he can make us some of his great coffee. He has an espresso machine in his condo."

Alex nodded, wanting to take this chance to meet another of the murder suspects. They drove only about twenty more minutes, and with the top down and the sound of the traffic, talk was again difficult. Once, however, Vaz reached over and patted her thigh, flashing the smile of an accomplished womanizer. Indignant, she crossed her legs and slanted them toward the door. He didn't miss the move but merely smiled again, this time winking.

Thomas apparently lived in an extremely luxurious condominium. Vaz gave his name at the gate and was waved through to streets lined with palms and wonderfully smooth barkless trees trimmed into exquisitely neat shapes. They were like something from a fairy tale.

"What're those trees called?"

"They're coral trees. They're something, huh?"

"I love them. I've never seen anything like them."

They pulled up into a brick driveway. The condo was smooth café au lait stucco with a red-tiled roof. It shared one wall with its neighbor, but both dwellings were the size of small mansions. Walking to the door, she asked, "Vaz, are you sure we won't be intruding?"

"Thomas and I are tight, don't worry. I've told him all about you and the inheritance. He just doesn't know how much."

The doorbell pealed, and then Vaz used a key to let them in. He yelled, "Hey, Thomas, Sandy—I've brought Alex."

The entryway was painted terra cotta red with white woodwork and a parquet floor. A Spanish chest stood beneath what Alex recognized as a Toulouse-Lautrec painting. Copy or the real thing?

Down the stairs trailed a woman in her twenties who couldn't possibly be Benji's mother. She wore purple sweats and slippers. "Vaz, darling. I wish you'd given us warning. I'm a mess."

He kissed her smooth cheek and tousled her blonde hair. "You're always gorgeous, Sandy, you know that."

Her fair skin flamed at the compliment, and Alex revised her age even further downward. She had neat, regular features, a light tan, and hazel eyes. She wore no makeup. It was clear from her puffy face that she had been crying. Holding out a hand to Alex, she said, "I see Vaz has his usual impeccable taste."

"I'm not a girlfriend," Alex said with a smile. "Just the bearer of some news that I hope will be good. I'm terribly concerned about Benji's kidnapping. A friend of mine is a witness. She's the one who found the note. I hope all of this is going to end with Benji's safe return and life in prison for the kidnappers."

"Thank you. We haven't heard about the ransom yet. All our phones are bugged by the FBI, though," she said. "I'm afraid Thomas is vegging out in front of a Dodgers game. He'll be down as soon as he gets decent. Can I get you something?"

"Ever the perfect waitress," Vaz teased her. "Could you get me my usual? And do you have some biscotti?"

"One double latte coming up. Alex? I'm Sandy, by the way. What would you like?"

"May I just have a steamer?"

"Sure. What flavor? I have cherry, coconut, and hazelnut syrup."

Alex asked for hazelnut. They moved into the living room with its cathedral ceiling. It was all white, except for some artistically arranged driftwood on the mantel of the gas fireplace.

"Sandy works at the espresso bar. She still loves it, even though she and Thomas were married last year and she doesn't need to work."

"What happened to Benji's mother?"

"Social climber. She decorated this place. But she found another ride to the top, and left Benji and Thomas. My brother doesn't care about that sort of thing. He's devoted to Benji, Sandy, and his restaurant, in that order. I can't even imagine the hell he's going through." Vaz kicked at the deep pile carpet as though it were lawn. "I know how tough it is on me. The kid's my shadow. I'm supposed to be taking him to Costa Rica this coming winter. He wants to be a pro like me, and he sure has the talent." Vaz sighed deeply and walked restlessly to the window, looking out at the view from the hilltop down to the ocean.

"I had the impression that your stepmother is a social climber, as well," Alex said.

"Yeah. That marriage has only minutes left, I'm afraid. The whole trophy wife thing stinks." Vaz jingled the change in his pockets. "I don't know what my dad was thinking when he married her. None of us can stand Janet. My mom's dead. Breast cancer. It was really hard on Dad to lose her. They'd been married thirty years."

"Now that Janet knows about the money, she'll probably want a big settlement if they divorce."

"Dad won't give it to her. They've got an airtight prenup. George, who hates Janet, drew it up when he couldn't talk Dad out of marrying her."

Alex decided to get even bolder. "And you? How many ex-wives do you have?"

Turning around, he grinned like a pirate who has just found

where the treasure is buried. "None. I was smart. I've never married any of my girlfriends."

"But you've got two kids!" Alex said before she could stop herself.

"Gifts from my gals. They didn't want them, and I wouldn't let them get abortions. This is California, Alex. Untraditional families like mine are a dime a dozen."

Sandy entered with the beverages and a plate of biscotti on a tray. She set them on the glass coffee table which bore a brass bowl full of dried pomegranates. "Have you got this crazy family sorted out yet?" Sandy asked.

"I'm a genealogist," Alex replied. "Vaz and Thomas's family is straightforward compared to some of the knotty ones I've untangled." Then she added, "I shouldn't say that. I wouldn't be surprised if I still turned up some illegitimate heirs. Then there's Paul Mardian's murder—" She stopped abruptly.

"Murder?" A man had entered on bare feet behind her. He was shirtless with a small pot belly, a good tan, and wore pajama bottoms.

Thomas. Why had she said that about the murder?

"Tell them about the artifacts, Alex," Vaz told her.

So she explained about the robbery, murder, and provisions of the will.

"And I'm guessing you think one of us murdered a cousin who was dying of cancer to get our hands on some old Armenian rubbish?" Thomas asked, his tone aggressive, almost threatening. "And Benji? Where does Benji fit into your little scheme? You think one of the family kidnapped him, too?"

"Whoa," Alex said, marshaling her thoughts as quickly as she could. "It's not rubbish, first of all. They were very valuable artifacts. Second, I never said any of you murdered Paul or implied that your family was involved in the kidnapping. That's the police's idea."

She repeated the tale of Paul Mardian's search at Ellis Island and the hire of the Armenian genealogist who had found them. "He had no heirs. That's why he wanted to find you."

"Why do I get the feeling that you actually think one of us might have killed this Paul Mardian?" Thomas was really angry now, and he gestured sharply toward the room. "Does this place look like I need money? Do you want to come into the other room and see my home theater?"

Before Alex could answer, Vaz put a hand on her arm. "Calm down, Thomas. She wasn't accusing you. I can understand what she means. You see, we're not just talking money. We're talking billions. The guy was really loaded. I can very easily see one of our charming cousins doing the guy."

"Professor Henry," Thomas said flatly. "He would kill for that Armenian stuff."

"Yeah, for starters. Or how about George? I don't think that guy could ever get enough money. And he didn't get a pile from his old man like we did. Aunt Nancy's husband was just a parking lot owner, remember."

"What's John like?" Alex asked. "I didn't get a chance to talk to him much."

Vaz shook his head. "John is Mr. Nice Guy. He would never do it. He's made a mint doing landscape architecture for the Irvine Company. His whole life is Brittani and their three kids. Of all of us, he's the family man."

"I can't believe you guys," Sandy said with half a sob. "Here our son's been kidnapped, and you're speculating about your cousins!"

"Hey, here's a thought!" Vaz broke in. "What about Mary's husband?"

Thomas punched his fist in the air. "Score. Dr. Butter-Wouldn't-Melt-in-His-Mouth. Bradley, Mr. Beautiful Surgeon, definitely takes the cake in this family for the Most In Love With Money. He's dying to have a wing named after him at Hoag Memorial Hospital." His eyes lit up for the first time since Alex's arrival. "Did you know he's keeping company with the hospital administrator? A foxy lady if ever there was one."

"Does Mary know?" Sandy asked.

"She couldn't *not* know. She works there too, for Pete's sake."

"Why does she put up with it?" Sandy was indignant now.

"I don't know. Dennis needs a lot of care, so maybe that's it." Thomas turned to Alex. "Mary's son was born with a rare skin disease. But maybe this inheritance will change things for them. She won't need Brad's income for Dennis anymore."

Alex's mind was whirling with facts she was anxious to get down on her descendancy chart. "What's Mary's married name, anyway?" she asked.

"Holborne," Vaz said. Then he turned abruptly to Thomas and asked, "So how's it going, bro? Do the police have any leads?"

The man's expression immediately darkened. "Some girl got a clear look at the perps. She's the one who found the note."

"Must have been the girl I saw the police take out of the store. Red hair. Just a kid." Vaz rubbed his upper lip with his index finger again. "She told the police Benji was happy to see them. So it was people he knew. That really bugs me."

"It's the desperation that bothers me," Alex said. "Why not wait until he was off work? Why risk kidnapping him in the store with all those people there?"

Vaz looked at her as if she had just sprouted a new head. "It's you. It's got to be you."

Alex had a sinking feeling that was not new. Too many times, her arrival on the scene to dig into someone's family tree signaled disaster. Charles called her a catalyst for catastrophe. When she had arrived unannounced at Oxford, the woman he loved had been promptly struck down by a bus before she and Briggie had even checked into a hotel. He had blamed her for a long time. And now, Vaz and Thomas would blame her.

"What could Benji have to do with the inheritance? How could the two things be linked?" she demanded.

"You're the only new factor in the equation of Benji's life," Vaz said. Sandy and Thomas were silent but accusing. "Nothing else has changed."

"We didn't even talk to Benji! We didn't even know who he was!" Alex protested.

"And someone wanted to make certain you *didn't* talk to him," Thomas said with certainty. "And that someone had to be in our extended family. Someone in our family has a secret that Benji knew."

"We didn't telegraph ahead!" Alex argued. "No one knew we were coming. No one in that store knew who we were or why we were there!"

The atmosphere in the room felt like the charged air in Kansas City before a bad storm.

"Someone knew enough to kill Paul Mardian, Alex," Vaz argued. "Whoever that was also knew a pompous lawyer would be turning up here eventually."

"But what could that possibly have to do with Benji?" Alex asked. "For that matter, we don't know anything about Paul Mardian's death except that he was killed for the antiquities. Maybe lots of people knew about them. Maybe it was some random radical Armenian nationalist."

"Of which there can't be many," pronounced Thomas. "And we have one of our very own in the Mardian family. How did Paul Mardian find us?"

"He advertised in an Armenian magazine," Alex said. She did not like the way her theory was being taken over by one of her suspects.

"And who would be likely to read such a magazine and impersonate a genealogist?" Thomas demanded.

"Henry," Alex said flatly.

"If Henry had anything to do with what happened to Benji, I will twist his neck right off his shoulders. I've never been able to stand the jerk. He's always been the different one in the family—prissy and nasty. Remember when we were kids?" Thomas inquired of his brother. "We started calling him Hal, because we thought no one could *want* to be called Henry. He stole my baseball cards in retaliation and said he'd only give them back if we called him his real name. I mean, ya gotta think the guy has something major wrong with him."

Sandy spoke up. "He's the only one in your family who is condescending to me because I'm a waitress."

"I think old Henry has a fixation," Vaz said. "I'll bet if there was ever such a thing as Armenian royalty, he thinks he's descended from it."

Vaz stopped pacing and sat by Alex. He finally began drinking his double latte, managing to rub his mostly bare thigh against Alex's skirt. She moved a good distance away. Thomas finally sat down next to his wife and drew her into a neat package by his side. Suddenly, he had reverted to a honeymooner.

"I really can't say that I see how you're connecting the two crimes," Alex protested. "I can see him doing one or the other but not both. If he impersonated the genealogist, he would be getting an inheritance and wouldn't need to kidnap Benji for money."

Thomas looked at Alex hard and then inclined his head slightly toward his wife. But she wasn't dumb. "How do we know he didn't kidnap him to murder him?" Sandy said, tears starting in her eyes. "Because he knew something?"

"I think we need to kick you out, Vaz," Thomas said firmly. "Delightful though your visit has been. The doctor gave Sandy some sleeping tablets today, and she took one just before you arrived. I need to get her to bed."

Alex was apologetic. "Oh, gads. I hope we haven't stirred you up too much. Forget about all this, Sandy. Benji was probably kidnapped by a klutz who thought he was clever, and Paul Mardian was probably murdered by a neighbor. Don't fret, as my friend Briggie would say. I wish she were here. She'd get you right into bed with a hot water bottle."

"She sounds like a lovely friend," Sandy said.

"She saved my life," Alex told her.

"She likes speedboats," Vaz added.

"C'mon, Mr. Surf Man. We need to get out of Sandy's hair."

"So where're you staying?" Vaz asked once they were on the road again.

Alex told him.

"Got your own room?"

Just in time, she remembered not to mention Marigny. "No. I'm sharing with Briggie. And she snores."

"Then she's a heavy sleeper."

"You're crazy if you think I'd hook up with you, Vaz. I don't do that sort of thing, and besides, I'm engaged."

"I'll make you forget that Brit, just wait and see."

"Don't bother, Surf Man. He's my one and only."

Vaz dropped her at the entrance to the Hyatt Regency. Not even bothering with the elevator, Alex ran upstairs and down the corridor to her suite, where she pulled out the descendancy chart and filled in all she had learned that night.

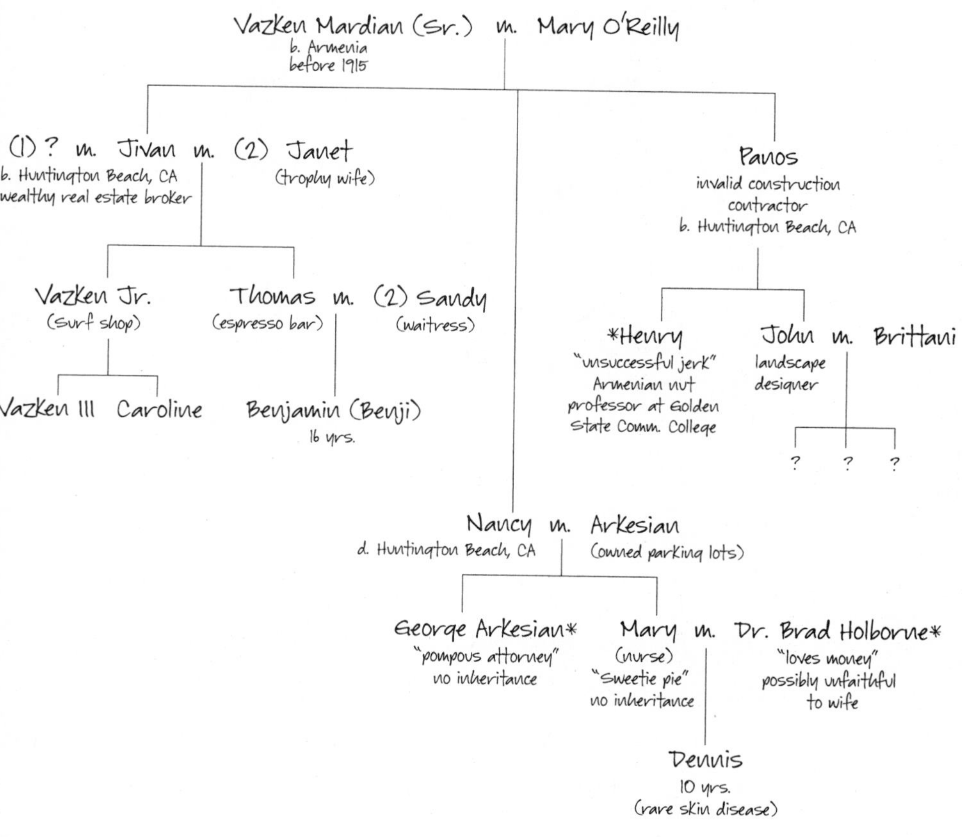

*suspected by Vaz Jr. & Thomas of Killing Paul Mardian

Chapter Ten

Only after she had finished the chart did Alex see the red message light on her telephone. The message was from an Agent Green, who asked her to call him whatever time she returned. When she placed the call, a man with a clipped, businesslike voice asked her to meet him in the lobby, even though it was ten-thirty.

A good-looking man of African descent with a trim black beard spotted her immediately sitting on the seashell couch next to the arrangement of lilies. He approached with a deliberate tread.

"I understand from Lieutenant Rhodes that you went to a little gathering of Benjamin Mardian's family this evening," Green said. "He gave me your descendancy chart. It's quite a crew. What did you think of them?"

Alex handed him the tape. "It's all there. You can judge for yourself. At least the main meeting. I went over to Benji's father's house with Vaz, his uncle. He said he'd talked to you already. I wish I could have taped their conversation, too, but I couldn't get to my recorder to turn over the tape."

"Anything interesting there?"

"Well, they've more or less narrowed it down to three people if it's someone in the family. One is George Arkesian, who is the son of Nancy Mardian. Apparently, she only married a parking lot owner, so he received no great legacy like his cousins. He's a self-made man, an estate lawyer. Vaz and Thomas say he's greedy."

The agent noted this on the descendancy chart he'd been consulting. Alex continued, "Henry is really disliked by all his cousins. They can't understand why he is such a fanatic about Armenia. Thomas and Vaz came up with the theory that he impersonated the genealogist that Paul Mardian hired to find his family. I assume Lieutenant Rhodes told you about the murder and the inheritance?"

Green nodded.

"Well, both Vaz and John think Henry is a perfect fit for the murderer of Paul Mardian, because he'd do just about anything to get hold of those Armenian antiques. He even speaks Armenian. And, as you can see from the chart, he's Panos's son. I guess Panos augments his income. I admit he's extremely obnoxious in person."

"Sounds like he's a probable perp for your murder. What about the kidnapping?"

"Well, I pointed out that he couldn't have done both. If he knew he was receiving a huge inheritance, he would have no reason for the ransom. But if he didn't do the murder, he might easily have been behind the kidnapping."

"Who's the third suspect?"

"Dr. Brad Holborne, a surgeon at Hoag Memorial Hospital who is apparently quite a player. No one knows why Mary doesn't divorce him. His dream is to have a new wing of the hospital named for him. I got the impression that he was terribly narcissistic."

"But pretty far down on the list of people who would have known about the antiquities, don't you think? And probably couldn't pass himself off as an Armenian genealogist. But he could be behind the kidnapping." The agent stared at the chart in his hands, squinting as though he could make out all the motives behind it. "Well, it looks like we have plenty of suspects. I'll move in on them tomorrow and see if they have any reason to kidnap Benjamin."

"I really don't know why anyone would have wanted to kidnap Benji. But I think they're all suspects for Paul Mardian's murder," Alex said. "Benji might somehow have been involved with that, or might know who did it." Her mind was speeding through likely scenarios. "That's the only way we could ever tie those crimes together. Maybe you should question his father."

"Ms. Campbell, I'm questioning everyone and I'm very good at what I do. Your part in this is over, and I really appreciate your help. Why don't you just enjoy your vacation?"

"Look how much I've helped you already, Agent. These people respect me, and I have a good reason for meeting them. They don't know I am looking for a murderer. I think they'll close ranks against you."

"Well, I guess you're old enough to know what you're doing. But keep in close contact with me, okay? I don't want anything happening to you or anyone else on this chart."

"Have you managed to keep Marigny Grinnell's sighting of the kidnappers private? Vaz Jr. knew about a redhead who witnessed the kidnapping and told his brother."

"I think I've kept her sufficiently anonymous. But the police are another matter. They've got the same problem most police departments have. Someone gets paid for leaking things to the press."

"There wasn't a policeman outside our door when I came back a while ago."

"I set it up myself with Lieutenant Rhodes. There's one there now. Now you go upstairs and get some sleep yourself."

When Alex got upstairs, she was surprised to see that the uniformed police guard was outside Briggie's door. He was also dozing.

Sudden panic took over. Downstairs at the registration desk, Marigny was listed as being in Briggie's room! Opening her door in haste, she found that the girl was gone. She went through the suite twice to make sure. Then she called Daniel's room.

"Daniel, is Marigny with you?"

"No. Dad and I are here playing gin rummy. Marigny was pretty tired after our little outing tonight. She wanted to go to bed."

"Well, she didn't. The sheets aren't even turned back. She's missing!"

Daniel slammed down the phone. Moments later, she heard hammering on the door. Both Richard and Daniel stood there. They insisted on going through the room themselves, as though Alex were incompetent.

"What's that policeman doing outside Briggie's door?" Richard demanded.

"That's Marigny's registered room. And he's asleep."

"We'd better call the police," Daniel said, his voice weary. "This is all my fault. I knew she would be in danger, being an eyewitness and all. I should have taken her home. Who knows where she is or what they're doing to her?"

Alex silently cursed the snitch in the police department. "I didn't mention her at all tonight. But an FBI agent warned me that there is a leak in the police department."

"FBI agent?" Daniel asked.

"Yes. They're on the case now."

At that moment, the telephone rang. A ransom demand? Alex snatched it up.

"Alex?" It was Marigny's voice, and she didn't sound the least bit traumatized.

"Marigny! Where are you?"

"It's all good, Alex, don't worry. I decided I wanted to do the scene here in Huntington Beach. I'm in Vaz's shop. I introduced myself to him when he got here a few minutes ago. He's helping me pick out a wet suit but thought I'd better call you and tell you where I was."

Alex had punched the speaker button so they could all hear, and Daniel shouted, "Marigny, you are grounded. Get back here immediately, without a wet suit. This vacation is over. You are returning to Kansas City tomorrow!"

"We thought you were kidnapped!" Richard bellowed. "I'm coming down to pick you up, and you had better be waiting out front of that surf shop so I don't have to get out of the van."

Alex felt as limp as cooked pasta. *Thank heaven!*

"If you two don't mind, I'm going to bed. Just remember she's sixteen, and this is a pretty happening place."

Alex fell asleep immediately and dreamt of Charles. They were flying, hands joined, over the dreaming spires of Oxford. The golden color of the spires, the round Radcliffe Camera, and all the college quads with their green lawns trimmed with flowers, drew her down with heartrending nostalgia. Then she was in the Christ Church college chapel with Charles. They were listening to the boys' choir. Her fiancé turned to her. "And you want me to give all this up?"

The phone ringing woke her.

"Alex? Is that little monkey with you?" Daniel inquired.

She called out, "Marigny? Are you here?"

No answer.

"I'm sorry, Daniel. She's not. She wasn't waiting for Richard?"

"No, she wasn't. And she wasn't in the store, either."

Alex woke Briggie by pounding on her door. Her friend answered almost immediately, rubbing the sleep out of her eyes.

"Marigny's missing," Alex said. "She sneaked away, and now look what's happened."

"Criminy! Alex, you're not thinking straight. How could those Mardians even know about her? This is just crazy! How would they even know where she was? Someone else must have her. Some pervert. Go take a cold shower and get your brain box back in gear."

"I don't need a shower, for heaven's sake. But you're right. She was talking to Vaz. Unless he called someone, they wouldn't know where she was. Neither would the kidnappers, even if they knew her name."

Vaz! Had he seen what happened to her?

Once she was dressed in jeans and a turtleneck, she ran down the stairs to the lobby and sought out her friends. Daniel and Richard had returned, and were ready to call the police.

"Daniel, did Marigny identify anyone tonight?"

"No," her ex-beau said. "The only blonde was sitting hip to hip with her husband. No blond surfer guys."

"That's true," Briggie agreed. "There weren't. Those guys must have just been hired muscle."

"She introduced herself to Vaz." Alex looked at her watch. Eleven-thirty. Surely Surfboards Unlimited would be closed by now. "Let's go pay him a visit." Then she remembered the only listing for Vaz had been his shop. She closed her eyes and shook her head in frustration. "Do you think he could possibly live above his shop?"

"I think we should leave this to the police, Alex," Richard said.

"But they don't know about Vaz!"

"So call them!"

"Give me the keys to the van, Richard."

"You can't go alone! Alex, what's wrong with you?"

"Marigny is only sixteen. She's been raised in the Midwest. She trusts people. Vaz is a lecher."

During all this conversation, Daniel had been sitting with his head in his hands. Now he looked up, angry. "Dad, if anything's happened to my daughter because of this case you dragged her into, I will never forgive you."

"I'll never forgive myself."

Daniel followed Alex out the door to the parking garage. "This is extremely weird, Daniel. No one in this group knew of Marigny's existence, much less that she could identify the kidnappers. Her name and everything might have appeared in the paper today. Agent Green said there may have been a leak at the police station."

"Marigny doesn't seem to have any sense," Daniel said bitterly, grabbing his dad's keys. "I've always known it would be her undoing."

When they reached the surf shop, Alex was grateful to see the light coming through the louvers covering the windows above the shop. Incredibly, Lieutenant Rhodes's Crown Vic was already there. After a few minutes of exploration, they found a back flight of stairs, entwined with bougainvillea. Hastening upstairs, Alex prayed that Marigny would be there and that she would be all right. Daniel knocked loudly on the inconspicuous door.

Vaz, in a sea green terry robe, his wavy brown hair mussed, admitted them solemnly. Daniel introduced himself briefly, looking around as though for signs of his daughter.

The lieutenant stood at the louvered blinds, studying the street below.

"She's the one who found the note, isn't she?" Vaz asked. "She was sort of freaked out by it. Wanted to tell me how sorry she was."

"What else did she tell you?" Rhodes asked.

"That her grandfather was the estate lawyer in the Mardian case and that he had brought her along for a vacation. Some vacation!"

"Did she tell you she saw Benji's kidnappers?" Alex asked.

"She told me. I told her that she shouldn't be advertising that fact."

The lieutenant broke in, "Where were you when you were having this discussion?"

"In my store, looking at the wet suits."

"Was there anyone around you whom you recognized? Members of your family, for instance?" the policeman pressed.

"Just my dad, Jivan. He was fed up with Janet going on and on about the money. He comes down periodically to see what I'm doing with his property and hassle me a bit."

"When did he leave?" Alex asked.

"Let's see. He was here when Marigny was making her call to Alex. I think he went down to Thomas's espresso bar after that. He may still be there. They don't shut down 'til one."

"Do you mind if I have a look around the apartment?" the lieutenant asked. "Or do I need a warrant?"

"What kind of creep do you think I am? I don't prey on young girls. I have one of my own." Then he sat in a chair and put his face in his hands, possibly trying to visualize what it would be like for him if Caroline disappeared. "All right. Go to it. Just try not to wake my kids."

Vaz's apartment looked like an adolescent's—surfing posters everywhere, decorative seashells on top of bookcases that held children's books, a lava lamp, a state-of-the-art sound system, and three surfboards leaning against the wall in the hallway.

But Caroline's room was furnished like a Barbie dream—canopy bed, pink carpet, flowered wallpaper. Her blonde head lay peacefully on her pillow. Marigny was definitely not there.

Vaz III's room was wallpapered with surfing posters, mostly of his dad. It smelled like dirty socks and looked like a dump site, but there was no Marigny.

"Well," Lieutenant Rhodes said, "you seem to be telling the truth. Can you give me your father's address?"

Vaz chuckled. "He's a curmudgeon. I'll give you his address, but I'd almost swear he's still at the coffee bar."

"Maybe he saw something," Alex said. "I don't think it's terribly likely that he kidnapped Marigny."

"Why don't you check out the espresso bar? She may have wandered down there," Vaz suggested.

"She wouldn't do anything so irresponsible!" Richard said.

When they arrived at Costa Rica Coffee, there was Marigny, gorging herself on biscotti and drinking a latte, telling Jivan Mardian the story of her short life.

Daniel, normally the soul of self-possession, exploded. "Marigny Grinnell! Don't you know the police are looking for you? Don't you know we thought you had been kidnapped?"

Marigny whirled in her chair, stricken. "Oh, Daddy! I'm so sorry. Mr. Mardian here said he'd keep an eye out for your car . . ."

"We came in the van," Daniel said shortly. "When you weren't there, we went home and called the police. We thought Benji's kidnappers had you."

"Oh, gosh!" Marigny looked almost green. "I'm so sorry, Dad, Alex. You must have been really worried."

"You should never have come out alone in the first place! What were you thinking?" her father demanded.

"I'm sixteen," she said stubbornly. "There were a lot of kids younger than me out walking around."

Jivan intervened. "It was not very wise, little one. Why do you think I brought you here to wait with me?"

The girl's eyes brimmed with tears.

"I suppose you've told him all about your adventure yesterday!" Daniel accused. "When are you going to learn to keep your mouth shut?"

"Daddy," Marigny said firmly, "Mr. Mardian is Benji's grandpa. He is really concerned. And what's more, I found a clue!"

"A clue?" Alex asked. "To what?"

"Mr. Paul Mardian called Mr. Jivan Mardian and told him about the will he had made. He also told him he was dying of cancer. The will wasn't the big surprise you all thought it was."

Jivan made a face. "It was, though. I never thought the man had so much money."

Chapter Eleven

Alex almost forgot to call Lieutenant Rhodes to tell him that Marigny was safe. The policeman was relieved but annoyed with the girl. Alex was so tired by the time she got back to the hotel, she couldn't even think of the ramifications of Jivan's revelation. She fell asleep on the hide-a-bed, after giving thanks that Marigny was safe.

She was awakened the next morning by the telephone. Struggling to consciousness, she hoped the summons didn't signify another disaster.

It was Charles.

"What a wonderful way to be awakened," she told him, snuggling down under the covers. "I miss you, love."

"What are you wearing?" he asked.

"Your crew shirt, of course. To tell you the truth, I might never wear lingerie again."

"My crew shirt is sufficient stimulation to my imagination, thank you. Have a heart and spare me black negligees, darling. It might overload and shut down altogether."

"What are you wearing?" she asked.

"Still in my tennis kit. I went to Frederick's after our tennis match and spent time with my nieces and nephews. Fortunately, they have no religious views. They're on holiday from boarding school. I hadn't seen them in ages."

"How did Hannah treat you?"

"Quite well, actually. She made a pitcher of Pimms and tried to convince me to partake. She really can't believe I don't drink alcohol. I never realized before how much the British drink. It's just part of everyday life. America doesn't have real pubs."

"You weren't tempted?"

"Not really. I had a gin and tonic without the gin. With a little lime, it's not bad. How's the case going?"

Alex took great pleasure in describing the Mardian clan but concluded with the news that part of the family at least had already known of their inheritance.

"Sounds like a rum bunch to me. The kind that believe in entitlements."

"Well, John and Brittani are nice. I don't think they're that way. I haven't met nurse Mary, but her brother George is definitely greedy, though I must tell you he's a double for Laurence Olivier."

"Remember, you don't like handsome men."

"I never used to, but there's this Brit . . ."

"Any other handsome Armenians?"

"Well, Vaz looks like a pirate. He wears his hair to his shoulders, and I suspect he shows off nicely in a swimsuit. He's determined to pry me loose from my fiancé."

"What are you trying to do? Give me an inferiority complex?"

"It wouldn't do you any harm, you know. Show you how most

of the world feels." Taking a deep breath, she said, "Okay, we've avoided the subject long enough. Have you seen your mother?"

"No. But I promise I will as soon as I shower and change."

"You're still worried about it, aren't you?" Alex's heart thudded.

"Well, I had a long talk with Frederick about the Council of Nicaea and the Nicene Creed. He was actually quite fascinated. But his interest cut out when I tried to explain about the Restoration. He's not interested enough to change. He hasn't got the need. He's quite comfortable with the Church of England and the way his life is going. Whenever Hannah gets too intense for him, he just takes himself off to a dig somewhere."

She sighed. "Charles, you would have been just the same if America hadn't shaken you up."

"You're probably right. My life was predetermined the day I was born. No one, least of all me, expected it to take such a radical turn."

"It must be very uncomfortable for your family. They probably don't know how to relate to you anymore."

"My mother's always been a pillar of the Women's Institute in her church. She practically runs it—very committed to charitable works. The Church of England satisfies her need for religion. I'm afraid that addressing the subject the way I did with Frederick won't work for her. She would see it as an attack on things she holds inviolable."

"Charles, don't worry about explaining things logically. That will never work. You've got to go against your natural instincts and speak about how you *feel.* She can't argue with your feelings."

"She'll be terribly hurt, Alex."

For that, she had no answer. Finally she said, "Have you prayed about this?"

"Well, no. Not exactly."

"Love, you've got to have the Spirit with you when you talk to your mother. You have to prepare yourself."

"That sounds kind of supernatural, Alex."

Her heart hit bottom. "Haven't you ever felt the Spirit, Charles? How did you know the Church was true?"

"I followed Moroni's promise in the Book of Mormon. I didn't have to think about it much. I just knew it was true."

"Well, start there, then. Your mother can't argue with that. Talk about Alma. I know how much you love him. Alma 32 always helps me if I have doubts."

"Thanks, darling. It's so soothing just to hear your voice. You might be right here beside me."

"The Lord can soothe you, too, Charles. Give Him a chance."

"I feel like a desert, Alex. I think I always have. My personal landscape is so predictable, so boring. You are the flowers, the butterflies, the oasis in my life. I miss you terribly."

"I miss you, too, though I can't put it in such an eloquent way. I find there are all kinds of little things that I want to tell you and share with you. It's like half of me is missing. Maybe I can fly over when the case is finished, Charles."

"Meanwhile, take care, darling. No coshing on the head this time, remember?"

"I'll try to avoid it."

"I wish I were there to watch over you."

"Well, I have my karate, not to mention Briggie, Richard, and Daniel . . ."

"My point exactly."

"Don't worry, Charles. I'm not the one in crisis. You are. I'm quite certain of my feelings, for once in my life," she told him, a bit more sharply than she intended.

"Alex, I'm certain all this can be worked out between us. You'll see."

"It's not you and me I worry about, Charles. It's you and the Lord."

"I understand. But please don't give up on me, darling."

"I won't. I can't."

"Daniel's turned you against me before."

"It won't happen again, I promise. Now, go get ready to see your mother, love."

Her fiancé promised to do that, and they hung up. Alex lay in bed, wondering what in the world she would do if Charles's testimony didn't survive the intellectual establishment of Oxford. But then she sat up in bed and ran her hands through her curls with a determined air. She had already decided, hadn't she? She would go over there. She would remind him. She had needed reminding many times when a new experience or eventuality had thrown her off-kilter. Last month, when he had been baptized, Charles had had no doubts. She needed to remember that.

Letting Marigny sleep, she took a shower. After she had French braided her hair to keep it manageable in the ocean air, she donned a gauzy turquoise and flamingo pink skirt, a turquoise T-shirt, and white flip-flops. Somehow, she was going to have to arrange a meeting with Mary Holborne and her husband, the only "suspects" she hadn't met, other than Panos, who had to be exempt because of his crippling injury.

Knocking at Briggie's door, she received no reply, so she headed down to the sunny dining room and asked for a table outdoors. The morning air was fresh and clean, and the ocean sparkled beyond, dotted with surfers catching the morning tide.

Once seated, she noticed Briggie and Richard at the end of the patio. The fact that Richard was holding Briggie's hand across the table and speaking with great earnestness made her duck behind the menu, hoping Briggie wouldn't see her. Obviously, Richard was having his say.

Just when she had ordered honeydew melon and an English muffin, Daniel sauntered onto the patio, dressed in white Bermuda shorts and his Surf City T-shirt that showed off his muscular chest and arms. Seeing her, he didn't wait for an invitation but sat down across from her.

"Don't look now," Alex said, "but behind you your father appears to be proposing to my best friend."

Of course, Daniel swung his head around to observe. Turning back, he said in a conspiratorial whisper, "What do you think she'll say? Am I going to have Briggie for a stepmother?"

"I seriously doubt it, Daniel. She's faithful to her Ned. And your dad isn't a member of our church. That makes a lot of difference to Briggie."

"Does that make a lot of difference to you, too? Is that why Charles was baptized in Jon's pond last month?"

"He didn't do it for me," she said firmly. "He did it because he believes that our church has Christ's restored gospel."

Daniel raised an eyebrow and looked doubtful. "Well, more power to him. I'd do a lot of things for you, Alex, as you know. But being dunked in a muddy stock pond is not one of them."

"That was Briggie's idea. I was surprised Charles went along with it. I would have been perfectly happy for him to have been baptized in a regular font in Kansas City or Chicago."

Daniel smiled. Though he wasn't classically good-looking like Charles, he had a tough wrestler's build, sparkling green eyes, and a killer smile. She had been unwillingly attracted by them once. Even now Daniel's presence made her feel safe and secure but a bit uncomfortable that he knew her through and through, as he proceeded to demonstrate.

"What are you worried about, Alex? It's something to do with Charles's rushing off, isn't it?"

"Good grief, Daniel! The man's mother had a heart attack. I would be more worried about him if he hadn't gone. It certainly wouldn't have shown proper feeling."

He ordered steak and eggs from the hovering teenaged waiter with the pierced eyebrow who had brought Alex her melon and muffins. Then he sat back in his chair observing her, his index finger pressed to his lips. "There's something else, though, isn't there?"

"I hate it when you do that, Dr. Grinnell. Get out of my head and mind your own business."

"How does Charles's very Oxonian family feel about his baptism?"

Daniel had been a Rhodes scholar, so she knew that he was extremely familiar with Charles's home ground. She also knew he could read her eyes, so she kept them set resolutely on the melon she was scooping. "Umm, delicious," she said when she had tasted it.

"Alex?"

Why did she feel compelled to answer him? "It's really none of your business, Dr. Grinnell."

"They think he's a head case, don't they?"

Resolutely lifting her muffin, she said, "I think you'd better leave and go join your poor father. It looks like Briggie's given him the bad news."

Daniel said, "Poor Dad. I sympathize. But he won't be put off easily, and I won't either. Not until your wedding day, Alex." Then he rose and went to his father's table.

Alex breathed a sigh of relief and finished her breakfast alone.

Vaz informed her when she telephoned him that Mary was home with her son, Dennis, who had a bad respiratory infection. She had called Vaz that morning to pick up some medicine that he was supposed to deliver. "Without Benji here, I've had to hire new help. The girl's not able to get here until noon."

"I'll take the medicine, Vaz. I want to meet Mary. Can you tell me where she lives?"

"In Corona del Mar." He proceeded to give her directions to the beach community.

This time when she knocked on Briggie's door, her colleague answered immediately.

"Alex, I just tried to call you! He went and did it!"

"Richard proposed?"

"Yes. At breakfast of all times. Before I'd even had time to get my thoughts together."

"You turned him down, I take it?"

"Of course! But I did feel bad. I tried to talk him out of it, to tell him how completely different we are. He even promised to go body surfing, if that would make me change my mind. Can you imagine?"

"Would it make you change your mind?"

"Are you crazy? Can you see me all gussied up, living in that big house in Overland Park? Going to fund-raising galas and, even worse, giving them? He clearly hasn't thought this through."

Alex differed. "I think he's had it on his mind a long time. Couldn't you live in your house?" When Briggie scowled, she said, "Are you still friendly enough with him to get the keys to the rental van? I need to take some medicine to Mary Holborne. Vaz was supposed to, but he has to mind the store. He can't get away, and her son is sick."

Briggie's look turned sly. "What's made you want to make her acquaintance?"

Alex shrugged. "Just a feeling that we ought to know all the players. I want to meet her husband, too. And there's nothing that says Paul Mardian's murderer was a man."

"Don't you think we should call on Benji's folks, too? Just to see how they are?"

"And find out if they've had a ransom demand yet?"

"Guess we're beyond foolin' each other. C'mon, girl, let's get going. We have a murder to solve. I've already got Richard's keys."

Chapter Twelve

Mary's house was perched on Spyglass Hill with a magnificent view of the Pacific. Covered in magenta bougainvillea, it looked inviting and cool.

The woman who answered the door, however, was much too thin, and her hair had begun to gray, even though Alex knew she was only in her late twenties. There were already lines of concern on her face.

"Hello, Mary. I'm Alex Campbell, one of the genealogists working on your inheritance. This is my business partner, Briggie Poulson. Vaz asked us to bring the medicine you wanted."

Mary Holborne sighed with relief. "I almost didn't open the door. I thought you might be selling something. Come in. It'll be lovely to have female company. Let me just run this up to Dennis. Make yourselves comfortable."

Alex and Briggie looked about them at a home that didn't seem to fit its mistress. It had the look of a museum. The floor was oak, the walls a pale golden yellow. The space above the black leather couch displayed an intricate Native American blanket in tones of black, gold, and orange-red. Native American antiquities were displayed on glass tables and ebony shadow boxes. Alex was certain the collection was very valuable.

Briggie said, "Are these supposed to be treasures?"

Alex said, "Very impressive ones, I think. Look, here's a real tomahawk."

"Well, glory be. My boys collected stuff like this all the time when they were growing up. Guess if it's worth money, I'd better take it out and send it to them. It's just mixed in with all their *Star Wars* action figures. I bring them out when the grandkids come."

Just then, Mary descended the staircase. She had something in her hands that looked like a very old leather book.

"I hate this place!" she said, noticing their interest in the collection.

She had run a comb through her wavy black and gray hair. Now she sat down next to Alex on the leather couch. Briggie reposed in a wing chair covered in a Native American print that Alex thought quite beautiful.

"The collection is your husband's?" Briggie asked.

"Yes. All our vacations are spent at native digs all over the hemisphere. Brad doesn't seem to understand that the dust and hot climates are really bad for our son's illness and allergies. Not to mention the living accommodations. Filthy tents."

Alex wanted to ask her why she went but thought the question too personal.

Briggie had no qualms. "Then why do you go with him?"

The woman had been kneading her hands into knots. "I've been doing everything I can to preserve my marriage. Even a really good nurse doesn't make enough money for the kind of care Dennis needs. He has Kawasaki disease, which is a skin disease that affects the heart.

Dennis has already lived longer than most children who have it." Then suddenly she sat up straight, and a radiant smile spread across her features. "But, thank heavens, all that is nearly over. I can take him to Mayo and get the very best care. He needs heart surgery. How long will probate take, do you know?"

Surprised at such a direct question, Alex said, "Mr. Grinnell can work pretty fast when he wants to. Of course, a lot of it depends on when he can get a court date."

"When Janet called the night before last and told me the size of the bequest, I actually broke down and cried. Brad, of course, was thrilled, but I told him right there and then that he needn't think he was getting his greedy mitts on it, that we were getting a divorce ASAP. Of course, he swore at me. He's never used any of his privileges to help Dennis in any way. He's amazingly unsympathetic for a doctor."

The memory of her triumph beautified her careworn face. "The gloves are off now, and Dennis and I are moving in with Janet and Uncle Jivan until the money comes through. I'm not putting up with Brad's affairs for another moment, now that I have money to care for Dennis and secure a future for him."

"You go, girl!" Briggie said.

"Is Brad likely to let the two of you go so easily?" Alex asked.

"He is embarrassed and repulsed by Dennis. He would have divorced me long ago but was afraid it would look unsympathetic for such a prominent doctor. If I do it, it lets him off the hook. I imagine he's got his trophy wife all picked out."

"Then why did he swear?" Briggie wanted to know.

"Because he wouldn't have access to the money. No doubt he had visions of becoming a researcher and setting up a world famous lab. It's so much easier not to deal directly with human beings, you see?

Unfortunately, surgeons are forced into intimacy when they cut you open."

Amazed at how much Mary was confiding in complete strangers, Alex surmised that she had kept her bitterness hidden for so long that she couldn't help but spew it out now.

"What's that you're carrying?" Briggie asked. "Is it something you want to show us?"

The nurse's face lit up once more. "It's a sort of emblem of my identity. I've been meaning to get it translated. I'm very proud of my heritage." She opened the book and smoothed its thick pages. "I was my grandfather Vazken's only granddaughter. He wanted me to have his mother's journal. He said it was the only thing he had left of her, since he'd been banished by his father for marrying my grandmother."

"What a treasure!" Briggie said. "How wonderful for you to have a piece of her life."

"I wonder if she tells the tale of her escape from the genocide," Alex said. "It could be an important historical document."

"Do you really think so?" Mary said, a note of caution in her voice.

"Henry knows Armenian!" Briggie said, her excitement obvious. "Would you trust him with it? You could finally learn her story."

Mary laughed. "I can tell you both are genealogists."

"It could have some information about your great-grandmother's family of origin. You could be one generation further back on your pedigree!" Briggie continued.

"Genealogy is basically detective work," Alex explained. "Briggie and I are sort of addicted."

Mary seemed a bit uncertain. "I hate to part with it, especially to Henry." She hugged the journal to her chest.

"Why don't you let us make a copy? We'll treat it with care," Alex said. "We're used to historical documents. Wouldn't it be fun to find out exactly what it says? I know I'd want to."

The woman looked from Alex to Briggie, obviously torn. "Okay," she said finally. "Between taking care of Dennis and my job, I don't have much time." Passing the leather volume over to Alex, she said, "Just take good care of it. Now, was there a reason you wanted to see me?"

"Well, we're trying to help the authorities locate Benji," Alex explained.

"Oh, yes, poor Benji. How can I help?"

"Well, we don't know exactly," Alex said hastily, and racked her brain for a suitable reason. "You see, Paul Mardian was murdered. Someone ruthless is at work here. Perhaps Benji could have recognized him or something."

"I seriously doubt it. It was probably local coke addicts or something. It usually is." Mary said. "That makes much more sense."

Briggie shrugged. "Maybe. But something tells me that the two events—the murder and the kidnapping—are connected."

"My friend gets these hunches pretty often," Alex explained. "Sometimes they're right and sometimes they're completely off-the-wall."

"Well, I think it's all very far-fetched."

"Has your brother said anything to you about the inheritance?" Alex asked.

"He was ecstatic. He called me today to tell me the amount. He's very fond of money. He drives a Maserati and lives in a custom-built home overlooking a golf course. But he's forever in debt."

"Well, that's certainly interesting," Briggie mused aloud once they were back in the van. "I can see George Arkesian killing our Paul Mardian with no trouble at all."

"Me too. Now, bearing that in mind, I think Thomas and Sandy live pretty close. Their condo is across from a huge shopping plaza called Fashion Island. Oh, that's it ahead."

Thomas and Sandy seemed to be holding court. Outside their condo was what looked to be a government-issue gray car and Vaz's BMW.

When Sandy opened the door, she was beaming. "He's alive! Benji's alive! We got to talk to him on the telephone. All we have to do is pay the ransom!"

"If you don't mind my asking," Briggie said, "how much is that?"

"Only fifty million!" Sandy said in tones of relief.

Alex looked at Briggie and saw her own astonishment mirrored in her friend's face. She hadn't been sarcastic. It would seem that she honestly thought fifty million dollars was small change.

Sandy insisted that they come in. "The FBI are here. They're going through Benji's stuff in his room, looking for clues."

"I'm so relieved Benji is okay, Sandy. This is my business partner, Briggie. Briggie, this is Thomas's wife, Sandy."

Just as they entered, Agent Green came downstairs. Alex was immediately struck by his aura of self-importance. "Have you any idea what this is, ma'am?" He held what looked like a pottery fragment in his hand. It resembled something like a primitive animal god. "It's a strange thing to find in a sixteen-year-old's room."

Sandy examined it. "Oh, that. My husband's father gave that to Benji as a token of his heritage. It's an Armenian artifact. Very old." She thought for a moment. "You know, Benji never said where his grandfather got it. Could it be that this Paul Mardian sent it to him? That it was one of those antiquities he had?"

Briggie spoke up at once. "I knew the cases were connected! Obviously, Benji must have known about the inheritance. I'll bet you anything Jivan told him!" She stopped abruptly, seeing where this would take her. "But that would make Jivan the murderer and the kidnapper, and he never would have kidnapped Benji. So, it makes no sense." She paused and then seemed to pick up steam again. "Unless Benji told one of his relatives! He might have shown Henry the artifact, for instance. Henry could have gone to his Uncle Jivan and found out all about Paul Mardian's antiquities and gone back to Kansas City and tried to steal them, got caught, and ended up murdering Paul Mardian!" Her weather-beaten face gleamed with triumph at her theory.

"Briggie, you haven't finished thinking that through," Alex said gently. "What you say could be true, as far as it goes. But I think it gives Henry or whomever the motive to murder Benji, not to kidnap him for ransom."

Briggie scowled. "Aw, nuts." Then she amended hastily, "I didn't mean that. I mean, I'm glad Benji's alive. But what Alex says is true."

Thomas joined them. "Sandy, do you think Henry could have resisted the idea of all those Armenian artifacts? Benji *did* show this to him. Benji didn't know about the inheritance or anything, but I'll bet you dollars to donuts Henry tackled Jivan about the owner. He could have stolen Paul Mardian's artifacts and murdered him!"

Agent Green said, "We'll have to have a little discussion with Henry. Taking stolen artifacts across state lines falls within our jurisdiction. Not to mention murder."

"I don't think Benji showed his little trinket to anyone but Henry," Thomas said. "It's probably worth a lot. My cousin is a professor and positively crazy about anything Armenian. The idea of those artifacts would be really hard for him to resist."

"And Paul Mardian was leaving them to the local Armenian church," Briggie added. "Not the family. Jivan might have known that. It was probably because of this family that he was leaving them to the local church instead of his own in Kansas City. He probably wanted them to be available for the family to enjoy them."

"This may not have much to do with Benji's kidnapping, but all the descendants of my grandfather are coming into a huge fortune," Thomas told him, ignorant of Alex's disclosures to the FBI.

A tumbler clicked over in Alex's mind. *Descendants. Not their spouses.* Why hadn't she thought of it before? But there were too many motives floating around in this case. They could follow up on Henry once they had Benji back. For now, they needed to concentrate on the kidnapping.

"Agent," she said to the man beside her, looking into his agate-hard eyes, "I have an idea that might connect Benji's kidnapping with the bequest his family is getting."

The agent looked slightly dazed. Sandy suggested they move into the living room. There was a gas fire burning in the fireplace. Alex thought Sandy must have lit it for visual comfort in this cold white room of her predecessor.

She sat down next to the FBI man. "I don't know if I told you before, but Briggie and I are genealogists. We've actually dealt with the FBI before. A couple of months ago, as a matter of fact."

"It's amazing how many motives for murder can exist in a family tree," Briggie added.

The agent looked at Alex with a glance she was familiar with. She was going to have to earn her spurs again. "So what's this idea?" he asked.

"There are a couple of very greedy people on this family tree who won't be receiving inheritances. And believe me, the inheritances are huge," Alex said.

"Are you going to tell me their names?" he asked, a glimmer of resignation in his eyes.

"Mary Holborne's husband, Brad, for starters." She pulled the descendancy chart out of her carryall. "See? Here's Mary. She is the only woman in the direct line from Vazken Mardian. All the direct line descendants are to receive large inheritances. Mary is divorcing her husband, Brad, so he won't get his hands on the money."

"But she found out about the inheritance *after* Benji was kidnapped," the agent reminded her.

"True." Alex felt frustrated. There was something here. She could just feel it. "But he's been having an affair. Maybe he planned the kidnapping so he could get the fifty million dollars out of Jivan. I guess it could be completely independent of the inheritance. He still has a motive." Agent Green's eyes grew speculative. "Brad is very ambitious and wants to set up a state-of-the-art clinic for research. Do I need to spell it out further?"

"So you think he's holding Benji for ransom because he wants money he knows Jivan Mardian would put up for his favorite grandson. Maybe he even resents that Jivan hasn't done more for his son, Dennis."

"From what everyone says, I think he's pretty narcissistic," Briggie said. "I doubt he's spared a thought for Dennis, Agent Green. But you brought up an important point. Obviously, this points to someone familiar with the family's finances. I mean, it's not everyone who could come up with fifty million dollars."

Thomas intervened, "You've hit the nail on the head. He probably thinks he's owed it somehow and resents being left out. That sounds exactly like Brad."

As he said this, Benji's father clenched and unclenched his fists, flexing his substantial forearms.

"Interesting." The agent was studying the chart when his partner came downstairs. He had a slim, compact build and a face that was oddly reminiscent of John F. Kennedy's. Agent Green said, "Hey, Bailey, you've got to look at this. I think Ms. Campbell may be on to something. A motive."

Agent Bailey strode forward. "This is Ms. Campbell and her business partner . . . er . . ."

"Just call me Briggie." Then, turning to Alex, she said, "The same motive could apply to Jivan's wife, Janet. Does anyone know if he's talked to her about divorce?" she asked boldly.

"She'd have to be crazy not to see the way the wind's blowing," Vaz said.

"What about this John's marriage?" Agent Bailey asked. He was obviously a quick study. "The same could be said of his spouse."

"Solid as a rock," Vaz pronounced. "John's life revolves around his family."

"Even mothers have been known to commit crimes. His wife may have plans to divorce him without his knowing."

"I suppose anything's possible where women are concerned," Vaz said. "But I could swear that Britt is solid."

"Well, this is all pretty circumstantial. I think we need to see who picks up the drop," Agent Bailey said. Suddenly he smiled, looking more than ever like Jack Kennedy. Alex, being Alex, wondered if there was some kind of shared ancestor.

"Drop?" Briggie asked.

Thomas ran a hand through his hair. "A trash can on the Huntington Beach pier tomorrow night. That's what the voice on the phone demanded for Benji's return."

Alex said, "You can get your hands on the cash that fast?"

Thomas laughed without humor. "Dad doesn't believe in banks. It's an old Armenian trait. He likes his money where he can look at it."

"But are you actually going to use real money?" Briggie inquired.

"Nope, we're going to nab the man or woman before they can get away to look at it," Agent Bailey said, radiating confidence.

"But what if you don't?" Sandy asked, panic in her voice. She was rubbing her upper arms as though she couldn't get warm. "The person might kill Benji when he figures out he's been tricked."

"Relax, Sandy. The FBI know their job," her husband said.

Chapter Thirteen

When Alex and Briggie returned to the hotel, it was to find a note on Alex's door. "Join us for lunch on the terrace. D."

Alex realized she was starved for seafood. "It must be the ocean air, Briggs. I'm really hungry."

"Time you got some meat on those bones of yours. I'll bet they have good pasta here. And their desserts look like they're to die for. No hot fudge sundaes, but they've got a chocolate cake that looks mighty tasty. Maybe they even serve it with ice cream."

Alex remembered to grab Mary's leather notebook on the way out the door. She had promised to take care of it.

Daniel, Marigny, and Richard were enjoying clam chowder when they arrived at the table with two places saved for them. At the sound of the surf, Alex promised herself that she would take some time on the beach this afternoon. Right after she made the copies. She would lie in the sand and think things through. The case, of course. And Charles. Had he spoken to his mother yet?

"Heard any more about the kidnapping?" Richard asked. "I assume you were out grilling suspects this morning."

"The ransom demand has come in," Briggie told him. "Fifty million smackers."

Richard and Daniel whistled simultaneously. Marigny merely said, "Wow!"

Briggie then related their theory of the kidnappper's identity.

"Well, I could see right through that Janet," Richard said. "And I think you're right about her. She's the type that thinks she's entitled to lots of money. I've had a few women like that after me, believe it or not."

Alex was amused at Richard's transparent attempt to make Briggie see what she was losing out on by not marrying him. Her friend merely looked skyward and rolled her eyes at Alex.

"I'm much more in favor of Brad. He's a textbook narcissist," Alex said.

"And you do know all about narcissists, don't you, Alex?" Daniel said.

She couldn't believe what she had heard. "I assume you're referring to Charles?"

He nodded, his face sober. "Classic case. See it all the time. Thinks the world revolves around him and women are his for the taking."

Alex rose from the table, taking the journal with her and walking away. At that moment, she actually hated Daniel. He knew just how to exploit her weaknesses, but she wasn't going to rise to the bait this time.

She heard Briggie taking Daniel to task as she moved through the doors. On the way to get the journal copied, she'd grab a burger.

Walking through the lobby with its seashell tones, she wished ardently that Daniel would go home. Charles was *not* a narcissist. His male beauty had actually been a handicap to him in forming relationships. No one in their right mind would want to be loved only for their looks. Not unless he or she were a narcissist. A narcissist would take for granted that any adulation was understandable and that another person's devotion to him was all-encompassing. And Charles wasn't like that at all. He had a depth and intelligence that would make such relationships unsatisfying. Because of his devotion to his dead first cousin, Philippa, whom he couldn't marry, Charles knew about real love and all its layers of complexity. Daniel's psychology skills had always been off where her fiancé was concerned.

She still had the keys to the van, so, after asking the concierge the way to the closest copy store, she went on her way, threading through the beach traffic. It was a glorious day, with a slight breeze from the ocean blowing through the fanned-out leaves of the palms. People walking the streets wore a variety of colorful beachwear. Next to a woman in the briefest of bikinis strode her "sugar daddy," his balding head already red from the sun. Teenagers skateboarded or rollerbladed between pedestrians. Other young people, still coated with sand, carried their surfboards under their arms or on their heads.

What would it have been like to have grown up here? She found herself wondering. The Chicago North Shore had been stiflingly correct. Like Charles, she had been born into a rigidly predictable life. Of course, things had gone horribly wrong. But maybe, if she'd had access to the beach, she would have become a surf bum. Instead, she had taken refuge in her bedroom, reading endlessly—the Brontes, Jane Austen, and Victoria Holt. No wonder she had fallen in love with an Englishman.

Having reached the copy store, Alex went in and carefully copied Mary's document. The seams in the binding were giving way, so she proceeded with great care. The ink was so faded that she had to copy on the darkest setting, the result being scarcely legible. After a moment's hesitation, she made two copies, thinking that Jivan, the family patriarch, would probably like one. The copy would give her a good excuse to call on him, do a little discreet investigating of his divorce plans, and see if there was any more to the story of Benji's figurine. After collating and stapling the pages, she paid and left the store. When she got to the van, she stuck one copy in the side pocket of the van to be delivered to Henry for translation. The journal and the first copy she laid on the passenger seat.

She had reached the dark interior of the hotel's underground parking when the car window on the passenger side shattered all at once, and something whizzed by her face. Slamming on the brakes, she ducked instinctively, covering her head with her arms. Two more shots were fired. She felt a blast of pain in her arm and collapsed into the glass. Her hand felt like it was on fire.

Barely conscious and with eyes tightly shut against the pain, she heard the passenger door open. Then everything went dark.

When Alex returned to consciousness, she was in an ambulance screaming off somewhere at top speed. An intent young man with lashless eyes was fashioning what she recognized as a tourniquet on her upper arm, above the spurting wound.

"Oh, good, you're awake," he said. "The perp hit an artery in your arm . . ."

At those words, Alex passed out again.

When she next woke, she was in a recovery room with a nurse attaching a bag of what looked like blood to the IV access needle in her arm. "You want something for the pain, honey?" she asked. "I'll bet that graze on your hand is like fire. Hands are full of nerves, you know."

"Did I have surgery?" Alex asked.

"Yes. The doctor had to repair the damaged artery in your arm. He cut out the jagged edges and inserted some synthetic material to link up the loose ends. The way you were bleeding, it's lucky you survived. I'm transfusing you right now. This is the third bag. You lost a lot of blood."

Reluctantly, Alex said that she did need something for the pain. The nurse was right. Despite the bandage that made her hand look like something from a mummy's tomb, it was extremely painful. Her arm ached, but her hand screamed.

"Does anyone know I'm here?"

"We found your key card in your purse and notified the hotel. Were you staying with someone?"

Alex gave the nurse the names of her "family."

"I'll have someone make the call right after I get you going on some morphine. Briggie, you said?"

"Yes. She's my business partner."

When the morphine hit, Alex was instantly asleep.

As if in a dream, she felt someone holding her undamaged hand. "I'm so sorry, Alex," Daniel murmured.

Wanting to tell him it was scarcely his fault, she simply could not make her mouth work. Nor could she remove her hand from his. Her eyelids wouldn't even open. She fell back asleep.

The next time she awoke, she knew the morphine had worn off. Agent Green was sitting in the chair instead of Daniel.

"Hello," she said, still feeling as though her head was floating near the ceiling.

"You gave us all a scare, Alex," he said. "If it hadn't been for a tourist who took cover behind a car and called 911, you would have bled to death by the time someone else found you. That's the good news. The bad news is the tourist apparently fled the scene after making the call. So we couldn't get an ID."

She shuddered. "I think I prefer clonks on the head."

He laughed gently. "Your friend Briggie told me about some of your exploits. She was trying to assure everyone that you were heartier than you look. I never knew genealogy was such a dangerous profession. Who wants you dead?"

Alex tried to think, but her head was still muzzy from the morphine and the pain. "I haven't a clue. Killing me wouldn't accomplish anything."

"There is nothing you know that no one else knows? Something about the inheritance?"

"No, I don't think so. I've shared everything with Briggie and the others. Are they in danger, too?"

"I don't know. But I advise you to leave all this business with Mr. Grinnell and go home."

Alex bolted up in bed and instantly regretted it as her head went spinning. "Agent Green, what day is it? What time?"

"It's Wednesday. The day after you were shot, and it's about ten o'clock at night."

"Good grief! I've been out of it a long time. What about the drop? Did you catch the kidnapper?"

His face became grim. "As soon as we made the drop, a swarm of kids appeared out of nowhere and began hunting in that trash can. They grabbed the package and ran like blazes. Before we could stop them, they ran to a blue van on a side street. We got a make on the van, but it had been reported as stolen in East L.A. That's the Barrio. A drug gang war zone. That's where those kids came from."

"Oh, my gosh! Do you suppose that's where they're holding Benji?"

"It's a possibility. Maybe some gang knows about the Mardian fortune, but it's more likely they were hired."

"Like those surfers who kidnapped Benji." She thought a moment. "Someone is working very hard to conceal his or her identity."

"Maybe they think you know it. Maybe that's why you were shot at."

"You will continue your investigation of Brad Holborne and Janet Mardian, won't you?"

"They're both being tailed. There's not much else we can do at this point. Your friends are chomping at the bit."

"That doesn't surprise me. You'd better watch Briggie and Richard. They're a gang of two, and every single time we've been in a mess like this, they've managed to get into trouble."

"To hear them tell it, it's you that gets into trouble."

"Where are they right now?"

"In the waiting room. Your fiancé is there, too."

"Charles?" Alex perked up.

"A stocky redhead built like a wrestler?"

"No." Alex told herself that Charles wouldn't know yet, wouldn't have had time to make the flight. "I can't believe he told you he was my fiancé."

"I just assumed it. Doesn't say much for my deductive skills, does it? I saw your ring and his white knuckles and drew a false conclusion."

"Could you send Briggie in, please? If you're finished with me?"

A nurse poked her head in the door. "Time, Agent. I need to check Mrs. Campbell's vitals and wounds."

Alex sighed. "Agent Green, give everyone a thumbs up, will you? I want them to know that I'm okay."

After another dose of morphine, Alex was trembling on the edge of consciousness when something began teasing at her mind. Something she needed to remember. Something she needed to tell Agent Green. Then she fell asleep.

Chapter Fourteen

When Alex next awoke, it was morning. Briggie was gazing at her and holding her hand, her face worried and exhausted. As soon as she saw her open her eyes, she said, "Does it hurt, Alex? You're white as a sheet. And I don't like your taking all this morphine. It's not natural."

"It's not natural to be shot and lose half your blood, either. Thank heaven for that tourist, even though he didn't stick around. That's odd, don't you think?"

"Let's not think about that right now," her friend said. "How's your hand? I heard that it was scraped and embedded with glass shards. Must have hurt like blazes."

"It did. But it's better now."

"Okay. Do you think you feel good enough to take some bad news?"

Her mind raced. "Benji's dead?" she guessed.

"Not Benji. At least not that we know of."

"Well, who is it, Briggie, for crying out loud?"

"It's Charles's mother. She had another attack, a massive one this time. They couldn't revive her."

Her worst fear had been realized. Oh, Charles! What are you thinking? What will this do to you? Will you blame this on me? Will you blame it on the gospel? Alex dropped into a black hole.

Briggie must have read her face, for she said, "I shouldn't have told you while you were on the morphine, Alex. I'm sorry. It's a depressant. Charles will be back. You'll see."

"How did you find out?"

"I started calling Charles as soon as we knew what had happened to you. No answer. I left a message with the porter at Christ Church, but he didn't call back. Finally, I called the Radcliffe Infirmary. The nurse there told me that his mother had died."

"So Charles hasn't been in touch with you?"

"No. And I checked at the desk of the hotel, telling them you were in the hospital, but they said there were no messages for you either."

"So he didn't even call me, Briggs. I can't even imagine what he's going through. I can't seem to deal with this now. It's too big." Sinking back onto her pillows, she realized she was weeping. She didn't even have the strength to wipe away the tears. Her whole world was collapsing inward.

"What you need is some diversion. Is it okay if I send Vaz in? He's waiting outside."

"I don't want to see anyone now," she said. Thinking of Vaz in the waiting room reminded her of a caged tiger. "I hope Daniel has left."

"Oh, no. He's here for the long haul. Bringing everyone food."

Alex sighed. "I'd much rather see Vaz. But first, Briggie, why did someone shoot me? Was I robbed?"

"No, that Guatemalan horror of a carryall you take around with you was still there."

As soon as Briggie left, the weight of the news about Charles's mother crashed down on her, and she began to cry more earnestly. She knew she needed to drop everything here and fly to Oxford, but she didn't have the strength. And why had they had to learn about it from the hospital? The fact that Charles had not called was not a good sign.

She was twirling her engagement ring on her left, undamaged hand when Vaz entered with a bouquet of yellow roses.

He grinned at her, and she managed an answering smile. "How did you know that yellow roses are my favorites?"

"I'd like to say that I am a psychic completely attuned to your every desire, but the fact is that Briggie told me."

"Well, thank you. How are all your relatives?"

"Half of them are in the lobby. Seems you've made a conquest of the beautiful George. And John and Brittani are there."

"How're Thomas and Sandy?" she asked, unable to take her eyes off the tattoo on Vaz's exposed bicep. It was extremely intricate and she wasn't exactly sure what it represented. "Have they heard any more about the ransom? I feel so helpless and out of it here."

"Another drop is on for tonight. Eleven o'clock near the Surfer's Museum, which is out of all the traffic. It will be closed, so there probably won't be a whole lot of people around there. FBI's actually putting snipers on the roofs."

"Yikes. I hope it doesn't turn out that you get another swarm of kids."

"You know, Alex, we all feel real bad about this." He gestured toward her lying in bed. "Have you any idea why someone tried to kill you?"

"Not a clue, I'm afraid. It's really weird. And a giant hassle," she told him. "I'm going to be fine. In fact, I'm going to ask to be released. I doubt it has anything to do with all of you."

"Will you tell me why you're crying?"

She began pleating her sheet. "Charles's mother had a heart attack and died. I just heard. She was a wonderful woman. I want to fly to Oxford, but I'm stuck here." She reached for a tissue on her side table and blew her nose. "Now, tell me the story behind your tattoo. It's intriguing."

"I wouldn't have taken you for a tattoo aficionado. It's a reproduction of an ancient Armenian coin that my dad has. It was passed down to him by his father. I get it when Dad dies. It's kind of a badge of identity."

"I had no idea you were connected to your roots in any way," she said, wondering if she had misjudged Vaz. Could he have stolen the antiquities? To bring back to his father? For some reason, she didn't want to believe it.

"Armenians are always connected. Like the Jews. And Briggie says you're a Mormon. They were persecuted pretty badly, I've heard. Doesn't it connect you to your history? I mean, I'll always feel like I owe something to the people who died in our Holocaust. I owe it to them to keep their memory alive."

Alex was intrigued. She never would have suspected Vaz of such feelings. She had thought him merely a pleasure-seeker. "Do you mind if I ask you a personal question?" she asked.

"Shoot. I have nothing to hide."

"You seem to be pretty committed to family. Why didn't you marry your kids' mothers?"

"I was what you call a free spirit, and so were they. That was over a decade ago. They wouldn't have made good mothers. It was all I could do to keep them from aborting the babies. To be truthful, being a father has changed me. Maybe someday I'll find a woman to be a good stepmother to them. Are you volunteering? I'd like her to be like you."

"Why? You don't even know me!"

"There's something about you, Alex. I guess I'd call it substance. Your Midwestern values. Your religion, maybe."

"Well, sorry. I told you, I'm committed elsewhere. I think I am, anyway. My fiancé is having some struggles with being a Mormon. Unlike you, we are still persecuted. No one kills us or tars and feathers us anymore. They just spread lies." She paused, and the tears started again. "Charles's mother's heart attack was brought on by someone telling her we were heathens and lots of other garbage. I don't know if Charles can live with his baptism causing her death. He'll blame himself forever."

Vaz thought a moment, drawing his finger across his upper lip, a habit Alex was beginning to recognize. "Bad luck," he said finally. "I wouldn't have any problem with your being a Mormon, you know."

Alex couldn't help laughing. "*You'd* have an awful hard time being one, though. And I'd never trust you one little bit. You're a chick magnet."

Vaz grinned. "Who do you want to see next?"

"The doctor. I want to be discharged! There's nothing wrong with me now. I'm just a little tired. Marigny's father, Daniel, won't let me overexert myself. He's a real mother hen."

"That bugs you, doesn't it?"

Alex looked at her beautiful roses. Bringing them was something that Charles would have done. "He just won't let go. He keeps telling me I've made a mistake. That Charles is a player."

Why was she confiding in Vaz of all people?

"Well, as a player myself, I think I'd recognize another one. All joking aside, I think he's completely smitten. Of course, there's no telling how long it will last."

At that point, the doctor and nurse entered. "Good morning, Ms.

Campbell," said the young doctor with the receding hairline and big ears.

Vaz got up. "See you," he said.

"Thanks for the flowers."

He left her with a wink.

The nurse took her blood pressure while the doctor listened to her heart. When he stood up and re-looped the stethoscope around his neck, he said, "You know, you are an extremely fortunate woman. You very nearly died."

"I didn't know it was that bad," Alex said, unable to conceive that things could happen so fast. One minute she had been fine, and the next, she was almost dead.

"But the good news is that your heart is fine and so is your blood pressure. You don't seem to be having any reaction to the transfusion, so I think you can be discharged. You'll need to keep the bandages dry and wear your sling." Pulling a card out of his pocket, he handed it to her. "My nurse has made you an appointment for two days from now. We'll want to check for infection and change the bandages. In the meantime, no fancy dancing. Give your body a rest. It's been through a terrific trauma."

Briggie came in to help her get out of her hospital gown and into the clothes she had brought, a loose emerald tunic top and her black leggings. After expressing her concern in her gruff way, she said, "You know, Daniel keeps calling Charles's rooms at the college and leaving messages with the porter. I can't get over it. Last time he called, he said you had almost died. He's angry that Charles hasn't called back."

"I wish he hadn't done that. Poor Charles has enough trauma in his life right now. Daniel was probably trying to make up for being so nasty about him. Anything new on the case?"

"Jivan and Vaz have been haunting the waiting room. John and

Brittani and George were all here, as well. I think they've kind of adopted you. Now that you're being released, they're having a dinner in our suite tonight. They think what you need is some good Armenian food. Mary's a nurse here and she's been keeping us updated on your situation. She has given the okay."

"Mary! Oh, my gosh, Briggie! The journal! Her great-grandmother's journal! It's in the van, along with the copies. I promised I'd take care of it."

"The rental company came and got the van. I'll have Richard look into it. I'm sure they would have kept the stuff in there someplace, unless they thought it was trash."

Of course they would. Alex relaxed. "And what's the status of things between you and Richard?"

Briggie rolled her eyes. "He wants to sell his house, retire, and take me around the world."

Alex managed a smile. "What a great idea! But who's going to get you out of your messes?"

"That's the least of my worries. And who are you to talk about messes? Look at you, for crying out loud."

"This was *not* my fault. It has to be a case of mistaken identity."

"Are you ready to go, smart aleck?"

"Yep. Why don't you and Richard go after the journal at the rental place, and let Vaz or Daniel take me back to the hotel?"

Her friend tweaked her toes. "Take care, kiddo. Richard and I are on the case!"

Alex was more than ready for a nap by the time Vaz saw her to her room in the hotel. Daniel had protested at her choice of chauffeur, but Alex reminded him he had a daughter who was probably getting sunburned and possibly being preyed upon by good-looking California boys. Looking like someone had jolted him with electricity, he shot out of the hospital. Obviously, he had completely forgotten his parental concerns. She hoped Marigny would forgive her for the speedy arrival of her father.

Vaz left her at the door, for which the police had ordered a guard. "Promise you'll call me if you change your mind about our descending on you," he said. "It's kind of a thing for the family to gather when there's a problem. Between the assault on you and the kidnapping, our instinct is to get together. But you shouldn't suffer for it."

"It will be a good diversion from my problems."

Leaning toward her, he kissed her cheek and ruffled her hair. "Get some sleep."

When she hit the bed, she felt like she was falling down fathoms of spinning blackness until she hit a cushioned bottom. She had a fleeting thought of Charles just before she fell asleep. What was going on?

She was awakened only a short while later by the shrill ring of the telephone.

"Alex!" Briggie said, "That journal wasn't in the van! They swear it!"

"Oh, no," Alex said groggily. "I wonder what happened to it. It was priceless."

"I asked to speak to the man who came to pick up the van, Alex," Briggie told her. "He said there was nothing on the seat. He would have noticed. It's his job."

Alex closed her eyes tightly, trying to remember as much as she could. Had the papers slipped to the floor in the melee? She simply could not remember. Then, unexpectedly, she *did* remember something. It took her breath away.

"Look, before I passed out, someone opened the passenger door. What if they stole the journal and the copies! It's the only thing that makes sense. Why else would I have been shot? Someone was desperate to get hold of that journal, probably before it was translated."

"But who knew you even had the journal? And for that matter, what was in it that was worth killing for?" Briggie demanded. "Who even knew there *was* a journal, for that matter?"

"Mary could have told someone. There was nothing secret about it. But you're right. There must be something explosive in it. I can't imagine what it would be after all these years."

"Don't worry about telling Mary. Maybe we can get it back before we have to say anything."

"How? She is going to hate me."

When Alex next woke, it was to the news delivered by Marigny and Daniel that the Mardian clan would be arriving shortly.

Chapter Fifteen

Marigny was there to help her dress, fortunately, as Briggie had not yet returned for some unknown reason. "Could you please rummage around and try to find something marginally attractive for me to wear?" she asked the girl.

Marigny wore white shorts and a perky blue and white checked blouse tied at the waist. She had about a million more freckles from her time in the sun.

"Dad said to remind you that you could be eating dinner with a murderer and the person who shot you. He said one of these people is off his rocker. Pathological. You know Dad, he's always fussing. I can't believe anyone in this family would hurt you."

"It's hard to imagine," Alex agreed. "The more I see of them, the more I think there must be another explanation for everything." Except the theft of the journal. Who else would care? But she said nothing to Marigny about that.

"He told Grandpa that it's time we all left."

"And what was Richard's reply?"

"To mind his own business. Grandpa also reminded him the police were outside your door, and that we hadn't had our vacation yet. I know he secretly wants to solve all this mysterious stuff with Briggie. He's really a different person with her, isn't he?"

"Yes, and it drives your father to distraction. Actually, if you don't mind, I think I'll attempt a bath. What time are the Mardians coming?"

"Around six o'clock," Marigny said.

"There's still a policeman outside my door, isn't there?"

"Yes."

"Then why don't you tell your dad to toodle along to his own room and come back for dinner?"

The bath was heaven. The hotel had provided bubbles. Marigny scrubbed her back, being careful not to get the bandages wet. "Dad is too much to take sometimes. Where is Charles?"

"I actually have no idea."

"We were all so worried about you. Who do you think is trying to kill you?"

"I have no idea about that, either. Nor who kidnapped Benji or why. Nor who murdered Paul Mardian. I just wish I knew what the motives are. I wonder if there are one, two, or three perpetrators."

She dressed in a long-sleeved aqua tunic and black leggings and put her sling back on. Marigny French braided her hair for her while Alex tried to put on a bit of makeup. About all she could manage was lipgloss and a little blush. After this exertion, Alex was more than ready to rest, but she didn't go back to bed. She seated herself in the living room of the suite in the clamshell chair.

"Thanks for all your help, Marigny. Could you get me the telephone and the directory before you go get ready?"

"Sure, Alex."

After looking up Thomas's number, she called his condo to speak to Sandy.

"Hello?" Sandy's voice sounded weary.

"Sandy, this is Alex Campbell. I'm sorry to bother you, but I have been so worried about Benji."

"Oh, Alex," her voice warmed. "I heard you were shot. Who is doing all these awful things?"

"That's what I'm trying to figure out. Vaz said you'd heard from the kidnapper?"

"Yes. A note this time. Slipped into our mailbox. Written on a computer, I think. They are going to give us one more chance. This time the drop is in a less public place. The trash can outside the Surf City Museum."

"That's what he said. Where's that?"

"A couple of blocks past Vaz's shop and around the corner. This time the money will be real, but the FBI is going to have snipers on the nearby roofs, and cars on each route out of here toward the freeway."

"That sounds like a good plan. I imagine they'll be careful to wound and not kill, since we have no idea where Benji is. I'd love to be a fly on the wall. I hope they nail the guy. But I'll try to be patient. Please let me or Briggie know how it goes."

"I will, if I can remember to call. This is incredibly stressful. Alex, I don't even know if the kidnapper will keep his side of the bargain. If Benji has seen him, he may kill him no matter if we give him the money or not." Her voice had escalated in pitch. "He may be lying dead somewhere in East L.A., and we may never know what happened to him."

Though Alex privately agreed, she tried to be bracing. "The FBI are really good at what they do. Put your trust in them for now. Okay?"

She was definitely *not* in the mood for garrulous Armenians, no matter how good their intentions were. One of them could very well be behind Benji's kidnapping. Brad or Janet? And who else would care about that journal enough to kill her for it?

Chapter Sixteen

Alex didn't know she had fallen into a doze until the door to the corridor opened and Daniel entered wearing khakis and a white polo shirt.

She had been dreaming a very confused version of *Pride and Prejudice* where Charles was Mr. Darcy and Daniel was Mr. Collins.

"Heard from Charles yet, Alex?" Daniel asked.

She stifled the desire to tell him it was none of his business. "I don't even know what time it is in Britain," she said offhandedly. "He'll call when he can."

"I left a message that you nearly died."

"He might not have gotten the message. He's probably staying with his brother, Frederick. I'm sure they're up to their necks in funeral plans. His mother was a pillar of her church."

"He didn't even call to tell you his mother had died!"

Alex pondered this. There was no way around that one. It was true.

"Look, let's not talk about Charles, okay? I'm very clear about what you think of him."

"Alex, I couldn't stand to see you hurt again."

She looked at his worried face and knew he was sincere. In her contrary way, that only put her back up. "Look, as soon as I've got my strength back, I'm flying over there. Charles is in a really difficult spot. His mother died because of his baptism. Or at least that's what he thinks."

"That sounds highly unlikely," Daniel said with a frown.

All Alex's anxieties came to the fore. "What do you know about it? Why do you even think it's any of your business? You hate Charles. But I love him, so everything you say is only causing me pain! Are you forgetting I just got shot? Why don't you get out and leave me alone?"

Daniel looked as though he'd been slapped. "Is that what you really want?"

"Yes," she hissed, all the while hating herself for losing control, for taking out on Daniel her worries about Charles.

He got up and went out the door. Marigny came out of the bedroom, her face concerned. "Why doesn't Dad understand that he only makes things worse with his confrontations? He's a psychologist!"

"Maybe he doesn't know how to deal with anyone who's not his patient and won't take his advice," Alex said, still angry. Then, realizing who she was talking to, she tried to control herself. "I'm sorry, Marigny. I shouldn't talk that way about your father. He's a good man."

The girl rolled her eyes. "Where are Grandpa and Briggie?"

"Who knows? Briggie said on the plane that someone told her about a great hamburger place called In-n-Out. Maybe they didn't like the prospect of Armenian food and decided to stop for dinner."

Not long after that the Armenians began to arrive. John and

Brittani were first, bearing an artichoke rice salad. Brittani looked spectacular in a gold caftan with turquoise stones adorning the placket and sleeves.

On their heels came Jivan with barbecued lamb shish kebabs and a wife who didn't look particularly happy to be there. Henry came, bearing nothing. George arrived with a date who was dressed in a navy blue suit and looked like she belonged on *Law and Order,* carrying a gallon of frozen blackberry yogurt. Mary arrived with an Armenian cheese pie and her doctor spouse, a blond and debonair man who reminded Alex of Richard Chamberlain. Vaz was the last to appear, bringing flat bread.

It took a while with all the buzz around her to realize that Daniel, Briggie, and Richard were all missing. Alex sent Marigny to her father's room to convey her apologies and collect him, but he wasn't there. Briggie and Richard were not in their rooms either, the girl reported.

"Oh, brother," said Alex. "Why do I have the feeling that something has happened to your grandfather and Briggie, and Daniel has gone to rescue them?"

"I think Grandpa secretly likes to walk on the wild side," Marigny said. "That's why he likes Briggie."

Alex tried to put her business partner out of her mind and do some constructive observation. Brad was making up a plate for Mary, staying by her side. He certainly didn't look like an about-to-be-divorced spouse.

Vaz made up her plate as Alex minimized her wound, reassuring everyone about her recovery. It was hard to believe one of these people wished her dead. When Jivan was certain that everyone had a glass of something in his or her hand (he'd gone back to the car for wine), he proposed a toast.

"To Alex. May she always be as brave as an Armenian."

When that toast was concluded, Alex raised her glass of tonic water. "To Benji. May he find his way safely home."

The crowd immediately sobered. The sound of the telephone ringing caused them all to jump. Marigny left the room to answer the bedroom extension. Alex sat rigid, her arm and hand throbbing, sure that Briggie was in some kind of trouble.

However, when Marigny came back into the room she was grinning. She walked to Alex's chair, patted her on the shoulder and said to the room, "Nothing bad, just a message for Alex."

As soon as they had resumed their conversations (except Jivan, who kept his gimlet gaze fixed on Marigny), the girl leaned down and whispered in her ear, "That was Dad. Briggie and Grandpa are in jail! They're waiting for the results of drug tests."

Alex couldn't help laughing. "Drug tests! What in the world did they do?"

"According to the officer who finally got them to pull over, which was pretty hard because Grandpa was weaving all over the freeway, when he saw his exit, he didn't look at any other cars but drove across four lanes of traffic, causing all kinds of accidents. The officer told Dad that Grandpa was driving like a big boat on the open sea."

"So, of course they thought he was drunk," Alex said. "As a matter of fact, that's your grandfather's trademark driving style. It works better in Kansas City."

"When he passed the Breathalyzer test, they thought he was high on something else. Briggie got real mad when they put him in handcuffs. Apparently, she mentioned her deer rifle and hit the highway patrolman on the back with her fists. So they cuffed her, too, citing her for 'impeding an arrest.'"

Alex shook her head. "Do you happen to know where they were?"

"They're in jail somewhere called Santa Ana. Dad says there are drunks in all the other cells. Briggie is real angry, and Grandpa is sulking."

"What's your dad doing?"

"Trying to convince them that Grandpa is an upright member of the Kansas, Missouri, and Illinois Bar Associations and that he will sue them for wrongful arrest."

"How long does it take to process a drug test?"

"The police want to keep them there overnight. Dad is on his way here. He sounds exhausted."

"Your grandpa has that effect on him." Alex laughed again, her wounds all but forgotten, and went back to trying to eat Armenian artichoke rice salad with only one hand and a plastic fork. In fact, she was very glad that Richard and Briggie had not gotten themselves into worse trouble.

Janet came over to stand by her chair, her plate containing a nice slice of Armenian cheese pie. As Marigny had predicted, she was overdressed in a sand-colored silk halter top dress with a string of diamonds around her neck. "Have you talked to Sandy today?" she asked.

Alex wondered whether she was a good actress or whether her question was as casual as it seemed. She decided on the former. Anyone who could deceive Jivan into marrying her had to be a sharp cookie. "No, I'm afraid I haven't," she lied instinctively. "Have you?"

Janet sighed dramatically. "She wouldn't take my call. There was an agent or something with her, answering the phone."

"Maybe she was too tired and overwrought," Alex said. "I don't have children, so I can't begin to imagine how I would feel in that situation."

"Benji isn't even hers," Janet said, thrusting her lip in a studied pout. Alex imagined she had picked up that trick from watching French films.

Alex said, "She feels as though he is. Even if she didn't, she loves Thomas, and Thomas adores Benji."

"I just wondered how the FBI was doing. Do you think they'll catch whoever is behind this?"

"I certainly hope so."

"What is their strategy?" Again, the seemingly casual question.

"I'm afraid I'm the last person who would know that," Alex said, praying that she sounded emphatic enough. "I'm not even a family member."

Just then, Brittani interrupted them. "Excuse me, Janet, but I wanted to ask Alex how she's feeling. This nutty family takes any excuse to celebrate with food. They claim it's genetic, but maybe it's too much for you."

"No!" Alex insisted. "I'm enjoying all this wonderful food. Or at least your salad. That's really all I've had to eat so far. It's a bit awkward with only one hand."

Janet drifted off in Brad's direction. Brittani whispered, "She's a barracuda. I wouldn't put it past her to have had Benji kidnapped for the ransom. It would be just like her. Jivan filed today."

"For divorce?"

"Yeah. John went with him. He's actually closer to his uncle than he is to Panos, his father."

"Is that so?" Alex asked conversationally. "I'd like to meet Panos."

"Why don't you come for lunch tomorrow? If you're feeling up to it."

"I'd like that. Maybe Daniel can take me. Would it be okay if he came, too?"

"Sure. Vaz says you're engaged."

"Yes, but not to Daniel. My fiancé, Charles, came with me to California, but he had to go back to England, where he's from. His mother just died."

"Oh, how awful! And you nearly killed! He must feel really torn."

"I don't think he knows about it, actually. I hope not. His family needs him right now."

"Well, we'll take care of you. How long will you be here?"

"I really don't know. We'd sure like to see this kidnapping resolved. And Richard needs to get documentation from everyone proving their identity before he can disburse funds." Alex decided to do a little investigative work. "Have you or John ever heard about the journal that Mary has? It's written by her great-grandmother, who came from Armenia."

Brittani frowned. "No. And that's odd, because John has always been interested in his genealogy, believe it or not. Not nutty about it, like Henry, but curious. Armenians are, I guess. I think it's because of the Diaspora. He's always wondered if there was more family around who escaped."

"Well, maybe she never mentioned it because it's in Armenian. I suggested that she get Henry to translate it."

"Hmm. What did she say?"

Alex told her of their plan, and how she was trying to carry it out when she got shot.

Brittani became very agitated. Her hands shook on the plate she was carrying. "All this violence is frightening. Who knew you had that journal?"

"Mary could have told anyone, I suppose. I haven't asked her. She doesn't even know it's missing. I'm hoping we can get it back before she finds out."

Alex decided to dig further. "Henry does seem like he has a chip on his shoulder."

"Yeah," Brittani said. "I shouldn't say it, but it would be just like him to steal those antiquities from Paul Mardian's house. And to panic and kill him. But it's never the obvious one, is it? Maybe it was that pirate, Vaz. He's staring at you right now. Pretty hard. I know that look!" She laughed. "You'd better watch out."

"Actually," Alex said with a forced laugh, "Charles is enough man for me. Even when he's across the pond." She paused and watched Brittani turn a speculative gaze on Vaz. Alex decided to switch subjects. "Do you think Brad might have had Benji kidnapped? Mary told him she wants a divorce immediately. She's moving in with Jivan."

"Hmm." Britanni considered. "That's a thought. I'll have to ask John what he thinks. He's been after Mary to ditch Brad, but she's always been so scared Dennis won't be able to get the care he needs. I can really sympathize with her."

"And now she doesn't have to worry," Alex said. "Dennis can live the life of a prince with her inheritance."

"I just don't know what I'd do if one of my children were born with a defect like that. Just about anything, I suppose."

"Even murder?" Alex asked, purely out of curiosity.

"Yeah, even murder."

At that moment, there was a loud pounding on the door. Alex cringed. They *were* making a lot of noise.

Vaz opened the door, and everyone gasped in unison. There stood Benji, grinning, flanked by two ecstatic parents.

"But you didn't make the drop yet!" Janet blurted out.

"I escaped," Benji said calmly. "I got the window unstuck in my room and took a bus and finally got a taxi the rest of the way."

Alex shot a quick glance at Janet. Shock had paralyzed her. But then, it had paralyzed everyone.

"Who was your kidnapper, son?" Jivan asked.

"I have no idea," Benji said. "Some surfer dudes approached me in Vaz's store. They said they were there to sign me up for an exclusive surfing invitational. When we went to the back room to discuss it, they pulled a gun on me and blindfolded me."

Jivan was at his grandson's side, hugging him to his long, powerful body. "What next?"

"We drove a really long way but not too fast. They stayed off the freeways, I think. Finally, we got to this stinking house. I think it was packed with illegals. They were expecting me, and they were paid to watch me. I had to eat cow intestines! Yuck!"

"Do you think one of them was your kidnapper?" Jivan asked.

"No. They were just paid to watch me. Some of them were worried that the police would bust them, and they'd be deported. While they were arguing and getting high, I finally escaped out a window that was nearly painted shut."

"We paid that taxi driver double. He drove all the way here from Whittier. It's surprising he picked Benji up, considering how bad he was looking," Thomas said. "Then we called off the drop. So, I'm here to tell you, if anyone here was responsible for Benji's kidnapping, there will be *no money.*"

Janet said, "What are you implying?"

Thomas gave her a flat stare. "Well, Stepmom, if you can't figure it out, then you're dumber than I imagined. Don't you know the police have been watching you?"

"And me, too, I think," Brad said acidly. "The devil of it is that you'll never know, will you, Thomas?"

Chapter Seventeen

No one stopped Thomas as he lunged for Brad. "You did it, didn't you?" Benji's father hit the doctor in the midsection with his fist. "You son of a . . ."

Sandy stopped him. "Thomas! Don't! He'll get you for assault!"

"I'll get those kidnappers to talk, then," said Thomas. "Benji knows where they live. I'll threaten them with conspiracy and get them all deported unless they tell me who they were working for!" Thomas's eyes were fierce. "So don't think you'll walk away from this, Dr. Holborne!"

The doctor just grinned. "No worries. I didn't do it. I wouldn't have hired incompetents."

That statement, Alex decided, was both cruel and true. But Janet? She might have hired incompetents. The problem was, Alex could not imagine her braving the ghetto in her designer clothes. Not unless she had a whole different side to her than Alex had seen before.

"I think your idea is a good one, Thomas," she said. "The FBI will insist on it. That's for sure."

"Yeah. We called them to tell them Benji is safe. They're coming by to depose Benji and give us a ride into East L.A. in a few minutes. He wanted to see you all, though, so they're meeting us in the lobby."

Benji gave a giant grin and high-fived his grandfather, who said, "Kid, you've made me proud. That was real enterprising. Just what I'd expect from a grandson of mine."

Thomas continued, "The gang may have scattered, but they're probably keeping an eye on their house. I hate to take Benji back there, but I want to nail these dudes."

"So do I," Benji said. "But for now, is that Grandpa's shish kebab?" The boy made straight for the food, while Alex marveled at his resiliency.

Had Janet had him kidnapped? Her remark about the drop not having been made was telling. Perhaps she had a fearless lover who had arranged things for her, but how would they ever know?

George managed to shake his date in the commotion and approached Alex's chair. "Have you got any idea who did this to you?" he asked, indicating her arm.

"None," she replied. "I was just pulling into the downstairs garage."

"Why in the world would anyone shoot you?" he asked, raising one handsome brow. "Was anything taken?"

She decided to lie. "No. Not a thing. Maybe one of your relatives doesn't like me."

"It makes absolutely no sense," he said thoughtfully, brushing wisps of her hair back from her face in an intimate gesture. "We're all thrilled with the news you've brought us."

"Well . . ." Alex said, "there is the little matter of the murder. Maybe someone thinks I know more than I do."

"Had you ever even met Paul Mardian?"

"No, but I've sure heard of him. Everyone has in Kansas City. He financed a huge amphitheater named after him."

"Hmm." He appeared to be thinking. "If anyone in the family had heard of that, I'm sure they would have looked him up. We've never heard of another Mardian in this country. What else can you tell me about him?"

"Well, he must have had kind of a sad life in spite of his wealth. He lost his wife and his only son years ago. I think that's when he started his Armenian phase."

"What exactly did he collect?" Alex was beginning to wonder if George was genuinely interested in Paul Mardian or in her. Holding his wine, he had squatted down so he was at eye level with her. His eyes were midnight blue and stood out against his tan. His smile was nearly irresistible. She remembered that he had been at the hospital after she was shot.

"Well, I'm not exactly sure. He gave Jivan a little pottery image from the collection. And I believe there were coins. The collection was said to be worth millions, so it must have been very old and very rare."

"I hope this isn't too personal, but I understand you are engaged."

"No. Not at all," Alex said. His eyebrows were raised in a query, so she went on. "My fiancé has had to go back to England. His mother was ill, and she just passed away."

This time his smile was a little wolfish. "I'd like to take you out while you are here. I don't know if your taste runs to opera, but we have a wonderful company here. They're doing *Tosca* at the moment. Say the word, and I can get tickets. I'm on the board."

What was this? Why in the world would he want to take her to the opera? She was sorely tempted, for she loved *Tosca*. But she had no clothes with her for such an event.

"I'd love to go, but I didn't bring evening clothes. Plus, I don't think we'll be here long, now that we've found all of you. Richard just has to prove your relationship to Vazken Sr."

"Don't you want to find whoever it is who shot you?"

She smiled. "You must be psychic."

"I can help. How about if I unobtrusively collect alibis? When were you shot?"

"You're assuming this was someone in your family? Why?"

"Who else do you know? Unless you think it was a random shooting, it must have been one of us. Nothing was stolen."

She was almost tempted to tell him about the journal but decided against it. "Okay. It was about two o'clock in the afternoon the day before yesterday. Just out of curiosity, why would you do this for me?"

"I've got a Sir Galahad complex. But now, I'd better get back to my date."

As he walked away, Alex felt she had never been so at sea about anyone in her life. She was convinced that he must want something in return. It made no sense, unless he truly was a nice man. She didn't know why that was so difficult for her to believe.

She just had one more thing she wanted to find out. When Marigny next came to check on her, Alex asked that she bring Jivan over to her.

The man approached her with what she imagined was his customary joie de vivre, now that his beloved grandson was restored. "What can I do for you, Alex?"

"The FBI found a weird little figurine in Benji's room when they were searching it. I just wondered if you knew what it was. It looked ancient."

Jivan shifted his feet and looked at the floor. "Well, I guess I'd better tell you that Paul Mardian sent it to me. He wanted me to have one of the artifacts. So, I did know about him before you came out here with the news of the inheritance. But I didn't know it was such a big deal, or that the figurine was really valuable. I gave it to Benji as a reminder of his heritage."

"I wonder if he showed it to Henry," Alex mused.

"Now that I can't tell you," Jivan said. "I really didn't mean to deceive you. It was just that when I found out the size of the bequest and the stolen artifacts, I thought you might make something out of it that wasn't true."

"You mean that you were guilty of the murder and theft?"

He looked directly into her eyes, his own clearly worried. "You don't think that, do you?"

"I don't know, Jivan," she said. "But I doubt that you would up and shoot me when you were obviously consumed with Benji's kidnapping. And I think whoever shot me was Paul Mardian's killer, although I haven't a clue what he meant to accomplish."

Jivan looked relieved. Smiling an attractive smile she hadn't seen before, he patted her good shoulder and gave her a kiss on the cheek. "I wouldn't shoot you, Alex. I'm glad you realize that."

What she realized was where Vaz had gotten his considerable charm.

Alex slept fitfully that night, even with the painkillers. At least she didn't have to worry about Benji anymore, but her would-be killer was still out there. If he were one and the same with the kidnapper, he had the journal, but what about the ransom? He or she had to be disappointed. Had the kidnappers even told their boss that Benji had escaped? If the bad guy was one of the Mardian family, he or she had had a nasty surprise when Benji showed up at her door. Her mind kept twisting the case around, but she could not make any of her scenarios fit. Especially when she thought of Gorgeous George.

At three A.M. the phone rang, just as she had finally dropped into real sleep. She knew it would be Charles. Her heart dropped. She also knew instinctively that at this hour, it was not good news.

"Alex?"

"Hello, love," she said. "I was so sorry to hear about your mother. How are you holding up?"

"Not too well, I'm afraid. How did you find out?"

"Briggie called the Radcliffe Infirmary. They told her."

"I'm sorry. I didn't mean for you to find out that way." Then he was silent.

"Charles, are you there?"

"Yes. I'm just trying to figure out how to say this next bit."

Bad, bad news. "You don't have to," Alex said. "I can figure it out." He had made up his mind. She couldn't possibly listen to what he was going to say. "Good-bye, Charles." She hung up the telephone and didn't answer it when it rang again and again.

Her entire body was catatonic. The only difference between her and a corpse was that she could see and hear. And feel, unfortunately. Perversely, or perhaps symbolically, the image of Stewart's plane bursting into a ball of flame and crashing into the earth revisited her as it always did in times of disaster. But the pain was worse.

There wasn't the period of blessed denial. There was only the pain slicing through her whole body, plowing up every bit of peace and wellness she had achieved in the years since Stewart's death. She knew that the new Alex was slipping away, and the old fearful, hardened Alex was taking her place. Trust was gone. Hope was gone. She felt bloodless, as though all the life were draining out of her just as it had two days ago. But there was no tourniquet this time.

If the gospel was true, why had it failed Charles? His voice had been dull, lifeless.

She couldn't even call Briggie, who was in jail, of all places. There had been a time when she would have called Daniel. But that was before last spring, when he had attempted to drive a wedge between her and Charles. It had almost worked.

Now she wished it had. Lying there, she couldn't even cry. Her body just became progressively more rigid. Sleep had fled.

What was she going to do with the rest of her life? She was thirty-seven. Had she lost her chance to become a mother? She couldn't imagine herself ever becoming vulnerable enough to love again. She would never cry another tear over a man.

It was this resolution that finally forced her to move her limbs. The clock said five A.M. It would be light soon. With difficulty, she got out of bed and dressed in jeans. Painfully, she pulled on her warmest turtleneck. After she had arranged her sling, she grabbed her carryall and her room key and walked out of the suite, careful not to disturb the sleeping Marigny.

Once out of the hotel, she walked toward the sea, crossing the almost-empty highway. She was barefoot and could feel the sand under her feet. That was good. Sensation was returning to her body. Walking toward the ocean, she heard the surf louder in her ears, drowning out the loop of her short conversation with Charles that kept replaying in her mind. Sunrise was tinting the sky pink. Walking parallel to the pier, she was surprised to see a number of surfers riding the waves. She stopped to watch them.

Gripped by a sudden reckless desire, she decided that she would break entirely with the past. She was an heiress. She would buy one of those little cottages on Balboa Island. Then she would buy a speed-boat, or perhaps she would learn to sail.

Vaz could teach her. She needn't worry about relationship complications with Vaz. She had known from the start that he wouldn't take anyone seriously. But maybe she could help him raise his kids.

If she wasn't traveling. When she had been married to Stewart, she had traveled all over the world, but she had seen it through his eyes. Now she was separate and had her own vision.

First, she would go to Tuscany. She would rent a villa and refine her drawing talents. When she had lived in Paris, she had become quite proficient with pastels, but when Stewart began taking her with him on his photo assignments as his assistant, she had never had time to develop that talent. Now, she had plenty of time. She might even take her mother with her. Amelia had rediscovered an old love of cooking that she had before she became an alcoholic. She was lonely in her North Shore mansion, and for the time being her MS was in remission. Alex could study the Tuscan light on the landscape, and her mother could explore the cuisine and even grow her own herbs.

While thinking these thoughts, Alex had strolled to the water's edge. The tide swirled around her ankles and she relished the fact that she wasn't completely dead to sensation.

Then, as though she had conjured him, Vaz appeared before her in a red wet suit, his surfboard under his arm.

"What are you doing up so early?" he asked. "Shouldn't you be taking it easy?"

"I'm planning my life," she said. "First, I'm buying a cottage on Balboa near your dad's. Can you teach me to sail if I help with your kids?"

"You're kidding, right?"

"Not in the least. In the fall, I think I'll take my mother with me to Tuscany and rent a villa. I'm going to brush up on my drawing skills, and she's going to do the cooking. I hate to cook."

Vaz looked at her closely. His hair was spiraling all over his head as it sprang from his wet scalp. "I know I probably shouldn't ask this, but you're sounding pretty crazy. Where does the Brit fit into these plans?"

Alex looked down at her hand where Charles's sapphire and diamond ring still sparkled. Pulling it off, she offered it to Vaz. "Here. Have an engagement ring."

"I'll keep it for you," he said cautiously, zipping it into a pocket on his chest. "If ever I saw a woman in love, it was you. You can't have changed that fast."

"I have. Cut everything off at the root." She tried smiling, but it was a weak effort.

"What happened? You look as though you haven't had a wink of sleep."

"I haven't, as a matter of fact. But you know what? I really don't want to talk about it. I've got the tourniquet snugly in place right now."

"Well, let's go to my place for breakfast."

"Fine. You can introduce me to your kids, and we can discuss this case. I'm so glad Benji is home safe. That must have put a spoke in someone's wheel."

Then, suddenly, Alex was crying. The strength left her legs and she fell into the sand like a puddle. The next thing she knew, Vaz was holding her and she was weeping into his salty wet suit. Not saying anything, he massaged her tense neck muscles and then moved down her back in a circular motion.

Just this small act of nurturing was enough to crack her brittle shell as though it were an egg. She was hearing Charles above the surf, *"But, Alex, you're my life! How can I leave you?"*

"I won't go without you!"

"You're my touchstone, Alex. I love you with all my heart. I don't want to be away from you. I don't want to lose you."

He had been desperate. As though he had known what was going to happen.

Then she remembered. She had been so sure she could win him

back if she just went to Oxford and fought for him. What had happened to that Alex? Was she going to revert to the emotional cripple she had been for the past twenty-three years? Hiding her heart where no one, not even her husband, could get at it? Was she going to refuse to risk getting hurt and lose the chance of eternal happiness? Did she believe the gospel was true? Or did she think Charles could shuck his testimony like a worn-out skin? He had sounded totally defeated on the telephone. Why had she hung up? Why hadn't she listened to his doubts and helped him to fight them? She should have been thinking about him, but she had been thinking only of herself.

Gradually, her sobbing ceased. Sniffling, she dried her tears with the back of her hand. She sat up, feeling renewed strength. "May I have my ring back, please?"

Vaz looked baffled. "You've changed your mind?"

"As soon as I've found out who shot me, I'm going to go to Oxford, and I'm going to bring Charles home."

Standing, she gave him a hug. "Thanks for your shoulder. Before you go back to your kids, can you answer a couple of questions?"

"About what?"

"Have you ever heard of a journal that Mary has that was handed down from your great-grandmother? It tells about the Armenian Holocaust, we think, but it's in Armenian. I had just made a copy to take to Henry to translate, when I was shot and it was stolen—oh, my gosh!"

"What now?"

"I wonder if they looked there."

"Where? What in the world are you talking about, Alex?"

"I put the journal and a copy on the seat. Those were definitely stolen after I was shot. But I also put a copy for Jivan in the little pocket in the door on the driver's side. I wonder if that was taken, too."

Vaz said, "Well, to answer your first question, no, I never knew about it. Why would it be important?"

"I can't imagine. But an even bigger question is, Why was it important enough to shoot me to get it, presumably before it was translated?"

"Someone must know what it says. Maybe it has something to do with the inheritance."

Alex twirled the ring on her finger. She was impatient. She needed to get to Charles. "I don't think that could be the case, because the inheritance was left to the descendants of your grandfather outright. The woman who wrote the journal wasn't even alive when you were all born!"

"You've got me, then," Vaz said. "But I don't think you'd better tell anyone else that that copy survived, and I think you'd better get it ASAP." He looked at his diver's watch. "I can take you as soon as I get my kids fed."

"That would be great. When we get to your place, I'll call. I think those rental places are open twenty-four hours."

Vaz's children resembled him. The daughter was dark-skinned with curly hair like Alex's. Her blue eyes stood out, magnificently framed by thick black lashes. She was unexpectedly shy, but her brother, Vaz III, more than made up for it. He had hazel eyes, and his head also was a mass of curls.

"Are you Dad's new girlfriend?" he asked.

"No. Just a friend. Your dad is going to help me solve a big problem. And maybe he'll even teach me to surf."

Young Vaz stood proudly in his ninja pajamas. "Did you know my dad is famous all over the world?" Running back to his room, he brought out a box. "See? These are his surfing medals!"

While Vaz made pancakes and Caroline set the table and poured juice, Vaz III lovingly displayed each medal—all of them first place from Australia to Central America, Hawaii, and the States.

Alex was impressed. It wasn't often anyone could follow a dream and succeed so well. Stewart had done it, too. His photographs were known worldwide. There was to be a retrospective in Edinburgh next fall. She hoped to take Charles to see it.

Once the children had eaten and were seated in front of the TV watching a DVD on whales, Vaz excused himself to take a shower. While he showered, Alex browsed through his magazines. On the bottom of the pile was one called *Binding Hearts.* She had heard the title somewhere, but she couldn't remember where. It proved to be an Armenian publication that had accounts of immigrants, firsthand reports of the Holocaust, and in the back a list of surnames. People searching for aunts, uncles, and cousins from whom they had become separated. Alex looked up Mardian and was surprised to see Paul Mardian's ad. "Looking for descendants of Vazken Mardian, born 1914, Armenia. Immigrated to U.S. in 1915." Following was his contact information. This must have been the ad that put Paul in touch with his cousins via the Armenian genealogist.

A chill went down her spine. Had this Vaz read it? It gave Paul Mardian's home address. Perhaps it was he and not Henry who coveted the antiquities. Perhaps Benji had shown him the little pottery image one day at the store. She had never considered that Vaz might be the thief and murderer. Had she been taken in by a charmer who was actually a snake? He had a fascination with the ancient coins. He had even had one tattooed on him. Perhaps he had gone to Kansas City, just to have a look at them. Maybe he hadn't intended to commit murder. Maybe Paul Mardian had a fragile skull, and Vaz hadn't known his own strength.

Vaz would be happy just to possess the coins. Maybe share them with his father. He wouldn't care about selling them or putting them on display. He would probably hand them down to his son.

She had to get out of here. Taking the magazine with her to show the FBI and Briggie, she got up and scrambled down the stairs to the street. A wave of weakness overcame her, the result of her sleepless night. She needed to get to the car rental place before Vaz. She didn't know for certain that he was behind the theft of Mary's journal, but she had no doubt that now that he knew of its existence, he would want it.

When she got to the hotel, it was eight o'clock. She hoped that Daniel hadn't left to pick up Briggie and his father yet. She pounded on his door.

He answered, completely dressed in khakis and a polo shirt. "Alex! Marigny just called. She was worried because you were gone."

"I went for a walk. Listen, Daniel, can I borrow your rental for about an hour or so? It's urgent. I need it right away."

"But you can't drive with your arm in a sling!"

"Well, then, could you drive me? I was shot because I had something someone wanted. A journal. I just remembered that I left a copy in the side pocket of the driver's door."

"Sure, I'll drive you. But why the rush?"

"I don't want anyone to beat me to it! C'mon! Let's go!"

"Okay. Sure. Let's just stop by your room and tell Marigny you're okay."

Of course, Marigny insisted on going too. "This is an adventure! I think I'm going to be a detective or a genealogist, Alex. It's so exciting!"

Alex thought Daniel might object; however, he grinned instead. "You've caught the fever, honey. Better watch out. Alex doesn't exactly live a tranquil life."

"Who wants a tranquil life? I want adventure! I was going to be a professional surfer, but I don't think I'm coordinated enough to be really good like Benji."

"Thank goodness for that, anyway," Daniel said under his breath.

Daniel's car was a medium-sized sedan, and fortunately he was an expert driver. They made excellent time to the John Wayne Airport's rental car facilities, even in the morning traffic.

"Can you imagine fighting this traffic every morning?" he asked Alex as he pulled into the lot.

"It's not my idea of a good time," she said. Then before she thought about it, she said, "Just lately, I've been thinking of moving to Tuscany for a change of pace."

"Where's that?" asked Marigny.

"Italy."

"What does Charles have to say about that?" Daniel asked, turning in his seat so that he could see her.

"We haven't discussed it," she said. "Now let's hope they haven't rented out the van yet."

They hadn't. According to the man behind the Avis counter, it was at a body shop being detailed. The body shop was in Santa Ana, the part of Orange County where Briggie was presently languishing in jail.

"Well, we can kill two birds with one stone," Daniel said. "Assuming Dad and Briggie are ready to be sprung."

Alex was angry at herself for making Daniel dash off without a telephone inquiry first. What if Vaz had made one, gone to the body shop, and retrieved the journal copy? The lack of sleep must be telling on her.

Chapter Eighteen

The body shop was a dive in what had to be the worst part of town. The proprietor spoke no English. Fortunately, Marigny had high school Spanish and after a while was able to make herself understood. They located the van, still missing its window, out on the lot. Holding her breath, Alex reached inside and retrieved the copy she had saved for Jivan.

"Oh, thank heaven! It's here!" She was so relieved as she folded the document and put it in her carryall that she left the proprietor a twenty-dollar tip.

"What is it?" asked Marigny.

"It's a copy of an Armenian journal that someone tried to kill me for," Alex explained.

"What are you going to do with it now?" Daniel wanted to know.

Alex had not anticipated this question. As Henry had to be considered a suspect with his all-consuming passion for Armenian artifacts, she no longer wanted to take it to him.

"I know!" she said suddenly. "The priest at that Armenian church probably speaks Armenian or knows someone who does."

"We have to go spring Briggie and Dad, so hold your horses," Daniel reminded her.

Sitting in the backseat, Alex was suddenly assaulted by a wave of overwhelming exhaustion. Without meaning to, she slipped into a sleep so deep that she didn't even awaken until they arrived back at the Hyatt Regency.

Briggie, looking more disheveled than ever, said softly, "Honey, what have you done to yourself?"

Alex, clutching her carryall, just said, "I've got to go to the Armenian church." But her arm was throbbing as though someone were beating it like a drum, and she was so tired any movement felt like she was making her way through molasses.

"You've got to sleep. It's only ten o'clock. I'm going to take a long bath, and then we're invited over to John Mardian's for lunch, Daniel tells us. You go to sleep. When your nurse finds out what you've been up to, all heck will break loose. Let's just hope she hasn't been here already."

At the door to her suite, she could only mumble, "Briggie, be careful what you say. The murderer could've been Vaz." Then she managed to get in and tumble into bed. Marigny came with a glass of water and four pills.

"It's ibuprofen. Dad told me to give it to you."

When Alex awoke, the clock said twelve-thirty and the home health nurse was bending over her, taking her blood pressure. "Seems fine," she reassured Alex cheerfully. "Now let's change that bandage. Your daughter tells me you have a lunch date, so we'll see how things are doing here."

Alex was so groggy she didn't bother correcting the woman's misconception about Marigny. She was profoundly relieved to find out that her sleepless night and crazed morning had done nothing to harm her wound.

"Does it hurt?" the nurse asked.

"Only if I do too much," Alex said. "Then I take ibuprofen and I'm okay."

"Well, that's good. I think it will be fine for you to go out to lunch. Just try to stay seated as much as possible. You don't want to elevate your blood pressure when that arterial graft is still so fresh in your arm."

Alex thought of her stroll on the beach, her mad dash from Vaz's, and the tension-filled drive all over the county. The graft had obviously taken, thank heavens. She hadn't given it a thought.

She hoped profoundly that Vaz would not be at the luncheon. She had no innocent explanation for why she had shot out of his apartment that morning.

Alex needn't have worried. As they pulled up to the lovely white clapboard two-story house with slate-blue shutters overlooking the rocky coastline of Laguna Beach, Vaz's BMW was nowhere in sight. Briggie, Richard, and Marigny preceded her up the wooden steps that wound through the flowering groundcover, while Daniel insisted on holding onto Alex's uninjured elbow.

Brittani greeted them at the door, dressed in a Hawaiian sarong, her blonde hair piled on her head. "I'm sorry, but when my brother-in-law heard you were coming, I couldn't keep him away."

Alex blinked and pictured the family tree. She must mean Henry. Good. She could question him about the journal. Their hostess led them through the house to the garden of tangerine-colored bougainvillea, palms, and masses of salmon begonias in back. Considering the premium on land in Laguna Beach, it was quite large. John saluted them from the grill, and a shrunken, balding man was lying on a chaise lounge.

"This is Alex Campbell, Papa," Brittani introduced her. "She's the one who got shot, as you can see. She's made the effort to come and meet you today. Alex, this is Panos Mardian."

"You'll excuse me, I'm sure, if I don't get up," Panos said. "Back injury. Will you introduce me to your friends? Who's that pretty young thing?"

Alex was willing to bet he was grumpy with a dry sense of humor. She replied, "That's my business partner, Briggie Poulson. Smile for the man, Briggie!"

Her friend chuckled. "Believe it or not, I was a pretty young thing once. And as a matter of fact, I just got engaged. This is my fiancé and the estate lawyer, Richard Grinnell."

Shocked, Alex was winded by this news. She could only stare at Briggie, who wore an air of coy innocence. Was she serious? Alex had a million questions but knew she must save them until later. "And this lovely young lady is Marigny Grinnell, Richard's granddaughter, who is here to learn to surf. We hope Benji will teach her. Marigny, this is yet another Mr. Mardian. Panos."

"That leaves only the wrestler," Panos said. "Would have liked to see if I could've pinned you in my day."

Daniel moved forward and shook the invalid's hand. "If it weren't for your back, I'd take you on now."

"There's a lot of things I'd do if it weren't for my back. My people don't like lying around. I've taken up chess and just recently started writing a family history. I would love to have met that cousin who left us the money. I'll bet he knew a lot about my grandfather that none of us ever knew. I'd like to have known the story of his escape from Armenia."

Briggie's little eyes lit up. "We can check out things like that. Maybe he belonged to a group that has archives in Kansas City or Chicago. His father was from Chicago, and Paul lived there until the eighties when he moved to Kansas City. I'd be willing to bet that there is some record of their story in one of those places."

"That would be great. Now, who killed my cousin and took his coin collection?"

He had addressed Alex. She replied, "Well, we've actually got three mysteries, and we don't know if any of them interrelate. And we don't know who the criminal or criminals are. Maybe you can be our armchair detective."

"The first two must be Paul Mardian's death and Benji's mysterious kidnapping. Does whoever shot you figure into the picture, too?"

"That's it," Alex told him, sitting down in a beach chair at his side. Daniel sat at her feet on the grass, while Richard strolled over to the grill to supervise. Briggie and Marigny wandered back into the house with Brittani, presumably to offer their help.

"Have you ever heard of a journal written by your grandmother Baydzar that was handed down to your sister, Nancy?"

"You know," the man said, screwing up his dark eyes, "I do remember when we were kids, she got this book in the mail. She didn't know what to do with it because it was written in gibberish. I wasn't sure, but when she showed it to me, I thought it might be Armenian."

"Well, it was. And she gave it to Mary before she died."

"Mary showed it to you?"

"Yes. It's her treasure. She decided she wanted to have it translated. I suggested making a copy and giving it to Henry."

"Oh, boy!" Panos rolled his eyes. "Henry probably would have died and gone to heaven, or wherever it is he's going."

"Well, it's gone missing. Someone shot me to get it."

Panos shook his head. "I hate to say this about my own son, but that's just something he'd do. He's a whack job. And I've been wondering about those coins, too. I thought he'd be pleased that they were left to our church, but he was madder than a hornet that they weren't coming to the family." He looked into Alex's eyes. "Do you think my son could murder a man?"

"I don't know Henry at all, Mr. Mardian. I've only met him once. At the time, he was over the moon about his inheritance. He said he was going to retire and go into research full-time."

"Don't know what went wrong with Henry," Panos mused. "He was a scrawny baby and sickly. Never liked sports. Always had his head in a book. Isn't interested in women unless they're Armenian. He's got some girlfriend up at the museum in L.A. Didn't have enough money to get married on, but now I suppose they will. She's a female Henry. Ph.D., scraggly hair, knock-knees, and glasses."

Alex looked around quickly to make certain Henry hadn't strayed into the yard. Daniel took no such precautions. "What do you think, Mr. Mardian?" he asked. "Do you think your son could've killed Paul Mardian?"

"If he'd been killed by a bullet, I'd say no. He wouldn't know what to do with a gun. But I understand his skull was smashed in from behind with something. That's just the kind of thing he would have done. Cowardly." The man who had been made old before his time looked profoundly sad. Alex thought she could detect tears in his eyes.

"Well, he couldn't have shot me, if he doesn't know his way around a gun," she said cheerfully. "Who would have done that?"

"Well, Jivan and Vaz go shooting on a range near here pretty often. But what would they care about an old Armenian journal?"

Alex felt cold inside. More evidence against Vaz. Why had she so instinctively trusted him when she knew he was the kind of man who wouldn't even marry the mother of his child? "Vaz takes a lot of pride in his heritage," she said. "That tattoo he has is copied from an old Armenian coin he got from his father."

"Then there's Benji," Daniel intervened. "Why would Vaz do something like that?"

"I guess no one told you, Daniel, but Vaz was with us at the time Benji was taken."

"But the kidnapping was hired out."

"Vaz doesn't need fifty million dollars," Panos said. "Jivan would let him have whatever he wanted."

At that moment, Henry stalked out on the lawn and went straight to Alex. "Mary said she gave you our great-grandmother's journal to copy and give to me. Where is it?" His voice was hostile and suspicious.

Panos said, "Cool down, Henry. See that sling on the young lady's arm? She's been shot. The journal was stolen from her. We were kind of wondering if you knew anything about it."

Henry looked as though he'd been shot as well. "Stolen? Stolen! It was priceless!" Then he accused, "You haven't told Mary! She doesn't know!"

Alex wondered about that herself. Why hadn't she told Mary about the copy? Because she'd fallen asleep. But she could have made a quick call before they left for John's. For some reason, maybe no more than Henry's bad manners, she chose not to tell him about the copy, either.

"Who would want it, Henry? Badly enough to kill me? I almost died, you know."

The skinny man looked taken aback. "I . . . I have no idea."

Panos said, "I think you were their main suspect until I told them you didn't know how to use a gun."

"Well, thanks for that, Father."

John's barbecued chicken was tender, juicy, and seasoned just the way Alex liked it. Brittani had assembled a large fruit salad with melons, berries, and sorbet. There were also sautéed red-skinned potatoes and grilled vegetables.

"Now," Brittani said gaily to Briggie, "Tell us when you got engaged. I want the whole story."

"My wife's a romantic," John said apologetically.

"Well, it's not terribly romantic, but we got engaged this morning about two A.M. in the Santa Ana jail," Briggie said. "We had adjoining cells, and Richard proposed through the bars."

Conventional Brittani burst into laughter, spilling her wine. Everyone but Henry laughed as well.

"What're your grandkids going to say about that, Briggie?" Alex asked.

"Not much. We won't tell them about the jail part. I try real hard to set a good example for them. Their parents worry they might take after me."

"Your children adore you," Alex said. "They wouldn't have you any other way." But she wondered what had changed Briggie's mind about the Church part.

"Well, as the only grandchild in question on my side, what do you think, Marigny?" Richard asked.

"I think it's a crack-up!" Marigny said. "A jailhouse romance. I'm just glad Dad's going to be around to get you out of trouble."

"He probably won't be," Alex said. "As I understand, your grandpa's going to retire, and they're going to go around the world."

The conversation proceeded with the tale of Briggie and Richard's incarceration and got increasingly more hilarious. Alex found herself wishing Charles were there. Daniel wasn't at all into the spirit of things.

On the way back to the hotel, Alex said, "Briggie, are you and Richard really engaged?"

"So far."

"Well, do you think you could manage to do a little job without getting into trouble? I'm exhausted, or I'd do it myself."

"Of course. I'm still your partner."

She explained how she had found the copy of the journal.

"Hallelujah! So that's why you wanted to go to the Armenian church. Richard and I can do it. Someone must speak Armenian in this community."

"That's just what I had in mind. Are you sure you're not too tired?"

"Nope!" She turned to her fiancé. "I'm driving."

"And I'm coming, too!" Marigny said.

When they dropped Alex and Daniel at the hotel, it was nearly four o'clock. Agents Green and Bailey were waiting in the lobby. Though she was tired, Alex was anxious to hear of any progress on the case.

"We have some questions for you, Alex," Agent Green said.

"Come up to my room." On her way to the elevator she asked, "What happened last night? Did you find the house where Benji was held? Were the kidnappers still there?"

"Just one. I think he was probably the only one with a green card, so he didn't have to worry about being illegal. When our car drew up, he took off running out the back door, but he was in pretty poor shape. He was an easy catch. At first he denied involvement, but when Benji appeared and identified him, he said he'd make a deal."

"Information for immunity?"

"That would have been too much to hope for on his part. Kidnapping is a felony. But he'll get a reduced sentence."

"So what did he say?" Alex asked impatiently.

"That's what I need to talk to you about. They only saw the man once when he came to him to make 'arrangements' for Benji's security. They have no way to contact him."

"So when Benji showed up here last night, the gang couldn't have let the kidnapper know he had escaped," Alex said.

"We've kind of built our theory around the perp being a member of the family. But I didn't want to take chances. We still had our men waiting at the drop."

"But no one came . . ."

"Someone came. About eleven-thirty. Dressed like a utility worker—all in gray, pushing a big bin. The men were only half expecting someone by then. It was a half hour late, and they knew about Benji's reappearance, so this guy sort of pulled the wool over their eyes. They didn't catch on until he started going through the trash instead of emptying it."

As Alex unlocked the door to her suite, she felt as though the world had turned upside down. "What? I can't believe it! That means whoever is responsible wasn't in my suite when Benji appeared last night. What did your men do?"

"They were a little gun-shy, in case this wasn't our perp. One of them just winged him in the shoulder."

"You have him then? What does he say?"

"No," Agent Bailey took up the tale. "The guy took off at the speed of light around the corner and into the crowd of people cruising and rollerblading down the main drag. Even at eleven-thirty at night, that place is hopping."

Agent Green looked apologetic. "It looks like we're back to square one, Alex."

Her mind felt numb.

"So how can we help?" Daniel asked.

"Did the man you caught give you a description of the man who hired him?" Alex asked.

"He wore a ski mask, but there were certain things that he couldn't hide. First of all, he was male. Next, though his hands were dark-skinned, he was hairier and more fine-boned than a Mexican. He thought he was probably an Arab—dark hair, dark complexion and eyes. That description would of course fit an Armenian. He had no accent. Another thing, he was skinny and very short. Only about 5'5". The agent flicked his notebook closed. "Do you know anyone of that description? Anyone you saw in Kansas City who was connected in any way with the case? Any random Armenian who is tangential to the Mardian clan—friends, that sort of thing?"

Alex felt deflated. "When you put it like that—a random Armenian—it could be anyone the Mardians know. I'm sure they have many Armenian friends who would know how wealthy Jivan is. They might even go to that Armenian Apostolic Church in Huntington Beach. Possibly, it was a job hired out. But, on the other hand, this whole kidnapping thing might not have anything to do with the murder or with who shot me. It could just be someone who wanted a slice of the Mardian money."

"Don't rule out Janet Mardian or Brad Holborne yet," Bailey said, smiling his cocky JFK smile. "They wouldn't be the type to brave the Barrio, I don't think. They would have had plenty of money to pay someone to represent them."

"It's all very confusing," Alex said. "Perhaps we should make a list of who could have committed each crime."

"I have one here that I made on our way back from East L.A. Why don't you take a look at it and see what you can add?"

"Okay."

Murder of Paul Mardian
Henry Mardian (motive: coins)
Vaz Mardian
Jivan Mardian
Brad Holborne (motive: money)

Mary Holborne
John Mardian
Brittani Mardian
Thomas Mardian
Sandy Mardian
Janet Mardian (motive: money)

"Okay," Alex said. "I hadn't thought of Brad having a motive, but you're right, if he thought he could get Mary to share the money with him. I still think Henry has the most believable motive. But they all have opportunity and means. You're right." Pausing, she said, "Plus, I found something this morning that could implicate Vaz." She pulled *Binding Hearts* out of her carryall and showed them Paul Mardian's ad. "If Vaz read this, he couldn't have missed it. It gives Paul's address and everything. Benji could have shown him the little pottery thing he got from his grandfather."

"Hmm. And you think he might have stolen the coins? He doesn't seem the type."

"He's kind of a closet nationalist. He's got a coin tattooed on his arm. But I agree. Henry seems far more likely. Whatever else he is, Vaz doesn't strike me as greedy." Something tight inside her relaxed as she said this. Perhaps in her overwrought state this morning she had jumped to conclusions.

"Look at the kidnapping now."

"The list's the same, except for Thomas and Sandy. And Brad and Janet are the ones with the motive."

"Now, your shooter."

"Everyone but Mary's on it, and no one but Henry's got a motive. If you can call it that. I mean, why couldn't he just ask? He's the only one with a motive for all three crimes."

"We're bringing him in."

"But his father says he doesn't know how to use a gun."

"Fathers don't know everything about their children."

"But how would Henry have known I had the journal?"

"Mary told us she called him."

"But why shoot me? I was taking it to him."

"Maybe he didn't want to give it back to Mary. Who knows? The fact remains, he's the only one who knew you had it."

Chapter Nineteen

"Look," Alex said, "I don't mean to tell you how to do your job, but don't you think it might be a good idea to find out what the thing says? I haven't had a chance to tell you, but I recovered another copy from the van."

"Well, that's a break," Green said. "But who do you know besides Henry who speaks Armenian?"

"Richard and Briggie are at the Armenian church now, trying to find someone. Just let me give them a call." She punched the number into her cell phone.

"Richard, this is Alex. Have you had any luck finding someone to interpret the journal?"

"We're just waiting. Apparently, one of the priest's older parishioners speaks and reads Armenian. As soon as confession is over, the priest is taking us to her house. She's quite elderly."

"Let the priest drive," she advised.

"He's too old."

"Can I talk to Briggie?"

When her colleague came on, Alex said, "So you haven't been arrested again, huh? Do you need Agent Green to see if he can expunge your police record?"

"I don't know. Being able to say I'm an ex-con would shake up the Relief Society a lot. But Richard got one heck of a ticket!"

"Do you think it will really make any difference to his driving style?"

"Not really. He's pretty set in his ways. And these danged freeways are so confusing."

"Well, you drive from now on."

"I wouldn't be surprised if Richard flew out here to contest the ticket."

Alex laughed. "Neither would I. Well, call me when you have something."

"Roger." Briggie hung up.

Agents Green and Bailey left to get a warrant for Henry's arrest. Alex thought their evidence was far too circumstantial and was much more inclined to suspect Brad or Janet of everything but her shooting.

She related this to Daniel.

"Why don't you leave it up to the police for once, Alex? This time you really came close to dying."

"There's obviously something or someone we're missing," she said. "That journal must have something pretty explosive in it."

They were silent for a few moments. The luncheon had tired Alex and she wondered why Daniel didn't leave.

"Are you going to tell me what's going on with Charles?" he asked. "You look worse today than you did yesterday. Did something happen?"

She sighed and closed her eyes for a moment. "He's given me

up," she said. "But I'm not going to leave it there. As soon as I've figured out who tried to shoot me, I'm leaving for Oxford."

"Was it the church issue?"

"Yes. His mother's death will be on his conscience forever, I think."

"Will you give it up to marry him?"

Alex looked at Daniel and sighed. "I would if I didn't owe my Savior so much. I know you think it was Briggie who rescued me in Scotland, and in some ways it was. But that was just the beginning."

"Tell me," Daniel insisted. "I really want to know."

"I can't tell you in any way you would understand, Daniel. It's no great mystery, but it requires an investment of faith. In the Book of Mormon it says 'a desire to believe.'"

"So your beliefs are more important than Charles?"

"It's not just my beliefs. It's Jesus Christ. His restored gospel. His atonement. If I put Charles above Him, it would mean Charles would be my God. And much as I love him, he is not my God. He can't save me. No human can."

"You've changed, Alex," Daniel said thoughtfully.

"How?"

"You actually trust someone. God. I never thought you would get to that point after everything that has happened to you."

She pondered this and wondered at it. "I guess I have. I don't know exactly when it happened."

"When you fell in love with Charles?"

"No. It had to be before that, or I never would have fallen in love. I wouldn't have let myself."

When had this miracle occurred? When had she forgiven God for all the abuse and abandonments she had suffered as though they had been His fault? An image came into her mind of her mother lying on the cot in the ambulance after she had almost died. It must have been then. She remembered seeing her mother as a wounded sheep on her Savior's shoulders, not as an ogre. It had made forgiveness possible. And once she had forgiven, her heart had softened and opened. It was really that simple.

Now, her heart filled once again with that redeeming love she had felt, causing tears to surface. In many ways, her life had begun that moment. She had been healed. And falling in love with Charles had been possible.

But what if Daniel had been by her side then instead of Charles? Would it have been Daniel she would have opened her heart to? Poor Daniel. He had been faithful to her for three years, and suddenly she had become engaged to someone else.

Looking through the window to the ocean, her exhaustion lifted. She owed Daniel an explanation. Maybe Charles would be obdurate. Maybe he would refuse to have her. Would Daniel still be waiting after all she'd put him through?

"Let's go for a walk on the pier, Daniel."

The blue sky and the sea breeze seemed like one puffy quilt, stitched down at intervals by the gulls wheeling up and down in search of fish. The scene anchored her so firmly to earth, it seemed unreal that she had almost died. She had been so involved in the case, so in and out of pain drugs, that she hadn't really let herself ponder on this matter. Had the Lord sent the Good Samaritan who called 911? Who was he? Why hadn't he stuck around?

The more she thought about it, the odder it seemed. He might have provided a description of her assailant. Or *was* he her assailant? The thought jolted her.

Then she began thinking about what would have happened if she had died.

"It's strange," she said, "to realize how close I was to death. Now that I'm emotionally whole, it's so much more important to me to stay alive. Even if things don't work out with Charles, for the first time since I was fourteen I have a real zest for living. I don't have that panicky feeling that some random meteor is going to sail into my life and smash it to pieces. I even feel that I might be a natural optimist, which is a surprise."

"There is no doubt that you're a completely different Alex from the one I met three years ago."

"I really never understood what it was about me that you found to love."

"As you have noted many times, I'm a sucker for a damsel in distress."

"I know. That is what drives me crazy!"

"I guess we're not really a fit, Alex," he sighed. "You've been right all along. Your independence drives me crazy. You want to live your life apart and separate. You don't want to share your emotions. An Englishman is a perfect mate for you."

"It's not that I don't want to share my emotions. I'm just not the needy person I used to be. The only way I can explain it is to say that I've laid my life, my future on the altar, Daniel. That's why, in spite of the situation with Charles, I can enjoy this day. I truly believe that there are powers and dominions we can't see that are watching over us. That's why I didn't die. When I just let go, and stop trying to control, I have a feeling of well-being that I've never experienced."

"That's powerful, Alex," Daniel said. "It's what I've always wished for you. What I hoped I could give you. Maybe it's better that you found it for yourself."

Alex inhaled the earthly smell of fish and seaweed and felt the salty breeze against her face. "Thank you, Daniel. Thank you for loving me and caring for me for so long. I don't really know how things will go with Charles, but right this moment on this pier in this sunshine, with you next to me, I'm not afraid. You'll always be dear to me, Daniel. Always. You and your dad and Marigny and Briggie are like family to me."

Daniel kissed her cheek. "Thanks for explaining it to me, Alex. I think I understand now. And I think I can finally accept that it's really over."

They were out on the balcony drinking ginger ale when the phone rang. It was Agent Green. "Have you any idea where Henry Mardian might have gone?" he inquired.

"He's not at home or school?" Alex asked.

"No. Was anything said at that luncheon today that might have tipped him off that he was a suspect?"

"Well, he's not stupid. Even his own father suspected him. And I don't think he's very brave when you get right down to it. Have you talked to his father?"

"Yes. He thinks he took off. You're right. Panos Mardian does think his son's a murderer."

Alex was not surprised. She tried to think where she would have gone if she were Henry but came up blank. "Well, I'm sorry I can't help you. He's not close to anyone in the family. He's sort of an odd man out. And until the inheritance comes through, he doesn't have any money."

She heard a long sigh on the other end of the telephone. "That's what his father said, too. Well, I guess we'll have to put out an APB on him. This certainly confirms his guilt in my mind."

Alex felt strangely uncertain about Henry's guilt, but his disappearance made her uneasy. Almost immediately, the phone rang again. It was Gorgeous George.

"Alex, are you free to have dinner with me tonight? I've dug up some interesting facts."

She looked at Daniel sitting on the balcony, sipping his drink.

He'd just have to understand that this was part of the job she had undertaken.

"I'd love to have dinner with you, George. But I need to be home fairly early. Doctor's orders." In reality, she was exhausted.

"We'll go to the Five Crowns in Corona del Mar. It's dressy casual. Shall we go early? About six?"

She agreed and then went to tell Daniel.

"Where is Marigny?" she asked. "Did she go surfing after lunch?"

"Yes," he replied. "She had a date with Benji. He starts work at Vaz's at seven. He wanted to take her to someplace local for hamburgers, and then she's going to help him tend the store. I predict I'm going to have a rebellion on my hands when it's time to leave."

"I don't think it's just Benji and the beach she loves," Alex told him. "I think she loves the whole Mardian family."

"Yes. She's very disappointed about you and me. She's ripe for her first serious emotional involvement. I don't know what I'm going to do about it."

"Don't fuss," Alex advised. "Let the Mardians be part of her life."

"If Benji gets his morals from his uncle, there will be real trouble, that's for sure."

"Oh, Daniel! Lighten up. If you're really worried, talk to Thomas and Sandy about it. I'm sure they don't want their son playing fast and loose with a sixteen-year-old girl, either."

"Good idea. If you're going out, I think I'll call and see if they'll meet me for dinner somewhere."

As soon as he left the suite, Alex began her preparations for her dinner with Gorgeous George. She decided on her dressy black slacks and a red cashmere turtleneck that she had only brought because Charles had given it to her for Christmas. She was glad she had it. She hadn't counted on the cool California evenings.

It wasn't until George called from downstairs that she realized

Briggie and Richard had not returned. She gave a quick call to Richard's cell. It went directly to voice mail. Either it needed to be charged, or he had it turned off. She hoped devoutly that they hadn't gotten into trouble again. Maybe they were looking for an engagement ring. The thought of her mentor with a diamond rock on her worn hand made her chuckle.

Her date had obviously come straight from the office. He wore a blue and white striped dress shirt, open at the collar, and navy blue slacks. His likeness to Laurence Olivier was even more striking than when he was in casual clothes.

She said the first thing that came into her head. "I wonder what you'd look like as an English Regency buck."

"Those were the fellows with the amazingly complicated neckcloths, weren't they?"

"Yes. And striped waistcoats and extremely well-fitted jackets. I think you'd look the part perfectly."

"Are you making fun?" he asked with a grin.

"Of you? I wouldn't dare!" she joked. "You're far too imposing!"

"Well, as long as we're talking periods, I think you belong to the Golden Age."

"You mean before the first World War?"

"Yes. With your hair in a Gibson Girl do, a shirtwaist blouse, and a black taffeta skirt with a bit of a bustle."

"That sounds fun!" Alex said with a laugh. "But I'd draw the line at a corset."

The Five Crowns was an elegant traditional restaurant that specialized in prime rib with all the trimmings. Charles would love it. If they were ever here together again, she needed to be certain that she brought him here.

There was a problem over the wine. "You don't drink? Oh, I was forgetting. You're on pain medication, aren't you?"

Alex let him think that was the case. As soon as she'd ordered, she asked, "Did you know that Henry has disappeared? The FBI went to arrest him, and he isn't anywhere around."

George swirled his wine around in his glass as he leaned back in his chair, perfectly at ease. "It doesn't surprise me. He's one of my two hottest suspects."

"Who's the other?"

"My charming cousin, Vaz."

This gave Alex a little jolt beneath her ribs. "You think Vaz shot me?"

"He's far more likely than Henry, actually. Henry I chose because of motive. You said you thought whoever shot you was trying to kill you because he thought you knew more than you should about the murder of Paul Mardian. That sounds most like Henry, because Henry would have made a deal with the devil for those antiquities."

"So why do you say Vaz is more likely?" she asked, slicing into her succulent and perfect prime rib.

"He's an ace shot. I'm assuming that you must have instinctively raised your arms to cover your head after the first shot?"

Alex put down her fork, panic rising inside her. "How did you know there was a first shot?"

George shrugged. "I guessed. I talked to the doctor when you were in the hospital. For the bullet to have hit your artery, your arms would have had to be raised, as though you were shielding your head. So that means you were expecting a shot. Therefore you had warning. A first shot."

Was he telling the truth, or was he the shooter? Would this evening out end with another threat to her life?

Chapter Twenty

Alex thought furiously. She must convince him she knew nothing about the murder of Paul Mardian and at the same time find out how interested he was in his Armenian roots.

"Well, that was a good guess. That's exactly how it happened."

He looked across the table into her eyes and grinned suddenly. "The legal mind has its uses. If probate law weren't so lucrative, I think I would have been a criminal lawyer. I love a good police procedural mystery."

"P. D. James?" she guessed.

"My favorite." He loaded his upside-down fork with food, like an Englishman. "Now, back to the case. Henry's lust for all things Armenian is pathetically obvious. But Vaz is shrewder. Did you know that he belongs to a group at our Armenian church that is putting together a white paper to present to The Hague on the atrocities?"

Another little bump in her midriff. This was not at all a comfortable meal. Suppose George's reason for coming to the hospital had simply been to see if she died or not? She was at a complete loss to explain it in any other way. And his sleuthing? Why would he bother to help her, unless it was to cast blame onto his relatives? She definitely should have waited for Briggie.

Still, the news about Vaz was unexpected. The more she found out about the piratical surfer, the deeper his Armenian interests seemed to be.

"No. I didn't know that about Vaz. It's surprising, I'll admit. But I have to tell you that whoever shot me was wrong about my knowing anything about that murder. I vaguely remember seeing a headline a few weeks ago about a billionaire dying, but I don't read articles like that. It didn't have anything to do with me, and they're too depressing. I had no idea I'd be looking for his heirs."

"Truly? You didn't talk to the Kansas City police before you came, or anything like that?"

"The first time I knew anything about the case was on the airplane, when Richard showed us his probate file. And when I woke up that morning, I didn't even know I'd be flying to California. It was a very last-minute thing."

"Do you usually rush off on trips like this on the spur of the moment?" He seemed to find this hard to believe.

"Quite often, as a matter of fact. Anyone who is in business with Briggie has to be prepared to leave literally at a moment's notice. But our business isn't to solve murders; it's to do genealogy."

"Then why are you still here? All the heirs have been found." George's eyes looked into hers with cheerful insolence, as though he knew she was lying.

"No one can legally benefit from a murder. I should think that would be obvious."

"So? Let the police or the FBI or whomever find the murderer." He drained his glass and, reaching for the wine bottle, poured himself a refill.

Alex was tired, as though she were in a fencing match with a highly skilled opponent. She tried again. "The sole reason for this dinner was that you were going to tell me about your little investigation into who shot me. It might interest you to know, if you don't already, that I came very close to dying. I'm not in a rush to get on an airplane right this instant. My wound is still being treated."

"That's strike two," George said flippantly, finishing off his Yorkshire pudding. "You've been all over creation with that wound today, wearing yourself out far more than you would sitting in an airplane seat."

"Have you been spying on me?" she asked, feigning alarm, which was in fact very real.

"I've been calling your hotel since early this morning. Where in the world were you at seven A.M.?"

"A walk on the beach. My arm hurts like crazy, making it difficult to sleep." Alex put down her cutlery once more and faced her opponent squarely. "Why were you calling me at that hour?"

He was nonplussed by her question. His first mistake. He should have expected it. She was growing more and more uneasy. Suddenly, she knew that his interest in her as a woman was completely feigned. His offer of help was an excuse to be "in" on her investigation. What was he afraid of? Why was he trying to turn her against Vaz? Did he know something concrete, or was he trying to move suspicion away from himself?

"How are you with a gun?" she asked.

He gave a slow grin. "Why would I shoot you?"

"You didn't answer me."

"I'm not as good as Vaz and Jivan, probably. But hunting is one of my hobbies. I turn out for deer season in Utah every year."

She squirmed uncomfortably in her seat. "Do you read Armenian?"

"Heavens, no! Unlike my cousins, I am completely assimilated." He smoothed his hair back and then shook it loose in a studied way, so a lock fell over his brow.

Alex wondered how any woman could ever be taken in by such an obvious narcissist. Suddenly weary, she longed to go home.

"Why did you ask me out tonight?"

"You intrigue me. So earnest. I get so tired of superficial females."

"I'm engaged, George."

"I heard there was trouble in paradise."

Alex pulled herself up and smiled with difficulty. "Nothing that can't be fixed. Now, do you have anything else to tell me?"

"Just that I'm here if you need me. I wouldn't count on Vaz, Alex. He's too much of an interested party."

She hoped he was wrong. In spite of herself, she was fond of Vaz.

When he finally delivered her back to the hotel, she said, "I'm sure you won't mind if I don't ask you up. I've had a long day, and my arm is pounding."

He grinned lasciviously. "I can be very gentle."

Choosing to ignore this, she asked again, "Why on earth did you call me at seven o'clock this morning?"

"To see if you were in your own bed. You weren't." Kissing her cheek, he left her standing in the lobby, outraged. She wished intensely that she could pin the entire case on Gorgeous George.

She wondered, suddenly, what Vaz would have to say about him. Forgetting her exhaustion, her wounded arm, and any danger she might be in, she did not go inside the hotel but walked instead to the boulevard and into Vaz's shop. She would be safe enough with all the crowds.

Vaz took one look at her and his face registered concern. Leaving to Benji the couple he was helping, he walked around the counter and came straight to her.

"What are you doing out here all alone? You ought to be in bed asleep!"

Looking into his concerned face, she wondered if he was merely a very good actor.

"Vaz, why would George try to call me at seven o'clock in the morning?"

Clearly taken aback, he said, "What? What are you talking about?"

He had hold of her good arm and was leading her out the door.

"Where are you taking me?"

"Just down to Thomas's. You need to sit down at least. Where did you think I was taking you? Does it have anything to do with why you ran out of my apartment this morning?"

"George tried to throw suspicion on you. He thinks you're the murderer."

"George is the biggest playboy in the universe."

Alex stopped on the pavement and stared at him. "What is it with you two? Do you have a contest going on or something? As I recall, the night we were out in your boat, you behaved the same way!"

"Hey, Alex. It's the singles' scene here. Where did you grow up? In a cave?"

She had never wanted Charles by her side more than she did at that moment. He had always respected her boundaries.

"You're the Neanderthal," she said. Then she turned and walked away.

Vaz called after her. "Let me take you home. You can barely walk, you're so tired."

"I wouldn't get in a car with you to save my life," she said and kept walking.

By the time she reached the hotel, she collapsed in bed, completely clothed, and didn't wake up all night long. She dreamt of the

Lady of Shalott at her loom, looking at life through a mirror. Probably because the complications of real life were suddenly too much.

The following morning, she was awakened by Briggie knocking on the door.

"I think I know who's been raising Cain around here!" her friend announced with a huge smile. Richard hovered behind her.

"You got the translation?" Alex drew them both into the suite and sat in a chair. Briggie's excitement was catching. "What did it say?"

"It's enough to make your hair stand on end. Poor Baydzar. You can't even imagine what she went through."

"Those Turks give even heathens a bad name," Richard said. "The atrocities . . . !"

"Richard, dear, don't inflict all that on poor Alex. Can't you see she's peaked? She can read about it later if she wants. It's enough for them to know that Baydzar's first husband, Dajad Mugerian, was a professor of Armenian literature. They had a son called Havsep in 1913." Briggie paused for breath before plunging on. "Dr. Mugerian was one of the first to be killed in the genocide . . ."

Alex's brain lit on the salient fact. "Mugerian. That name's familiar for some reason."

"I know. I had that feeling, too. Let me finish, even if you know where this is going. I've earned a little crowing time after a night spent in the hoosegow."

"Okay. Crow! But be quick about it!"

"You might think that Baydzar would have taken her oldest son, who was only four years old, with her when she and her second husband, Great-Grandpa Mardian, escaped with their two sons. Vazken and Hamazasb, remember."

"But she didn't? Why, for heaven's sake?" Alex demanded.

"It was apparently a very patriarchal society. When her husband was killed, Baydzar's in-laws, the Mugerians, took her in along with her son, Havsep. When she married Great-Grandpa Mardian, everything was fine until she told her former in-laws she and Great-Grandpa had to escape or he would be murdered by the Turks. Fortunately, they had an informant working by then who hid . . ."

"Briggie!"

"Well, the upshot of the whole thing was that they had to leave Havsep behind with his Mugerian grandparents. He was considered more theirs than hers."

"How horrible! Were the Mugerians in denial about the genocide or something?"

"Not for long. Baydzar had contacts in Armenia for a couple of years after they came to America. They knew how much she loved Havsep and kept an eye on him. Eventually, the Turks burned the Mugerians out of their farm, and they only just escaped execution by hiding—"

"Briggie!"

"Okay, okay. I just thought you might like a little human interest—"

"Later!"

"Baydzar's contact's last communication was that the Mugerians were headed for America."

"And that's all?"

"All!" Briggie looked affronted. "I think that's a lot. I even made a descendancy chart last night when we got home. I brought it to show you, but you weren't here."

Alex glanced at the rough chart. "I wish I could remember where I've heard that name. I've got too many Armenian names rattling around my head. Maybe it's just that it's so close to Mardian." Twining a piece of hair around her finger, she finally asked Richard,

"Could you do me a big favor and bring your Mardian probate file in here?"

Richard was very perky this morning. "Sure thing!" he said.

Marigny came out of the bedroom dressed in a green wet suit that Alex hadn't seen. "Benji and I are going surfing this morning before it gets too crowded. Then he's taking me and Dad out to lunch at his favorite Mexican restaurant."

"Okay, honey, have fun," said Alex.

Richard came in with the file as she left. Alex seized it, thanking him. It only took a few minutes to find what she was looking for. "Yes!" she exclaimed. "The 'genealogist' who worked for Paul Mardian was Leon Mugerian!"

"Glory!" said Briggie.

"Whoa!" Richard exclaimed. "Brighamina and I were sure that genealogy business was a scam. We thought it was one of these Mardians!" He slapped his knee. "Well, if that doesn't put the coyote in the henhouse!"

"It can't be a coincidence, guys. I think we've just stumbled on a hidden branch of the family."

Alex sat staring out the window at the ocean, putting together all the various pieces of the Mardian puzzle. Finally, she said, "How about this? Somehow this modern-day Mugerian knew the journal would expose him. He probably did the murder for the coins. He's probably as much of an Armenian chauvinist as Henry."

Richard said, "I don't want to rain on your parade, but how in the world would he even know that the journal existed, or what it said, or that you had it?"

"That does present a big problem," Alex admitted.

"There's another problem," Briggie said. "How did Mugerian get hooked up with Paul Mardian in the first place?"

"We're missing some pieces," Alex admitted. "But there is a

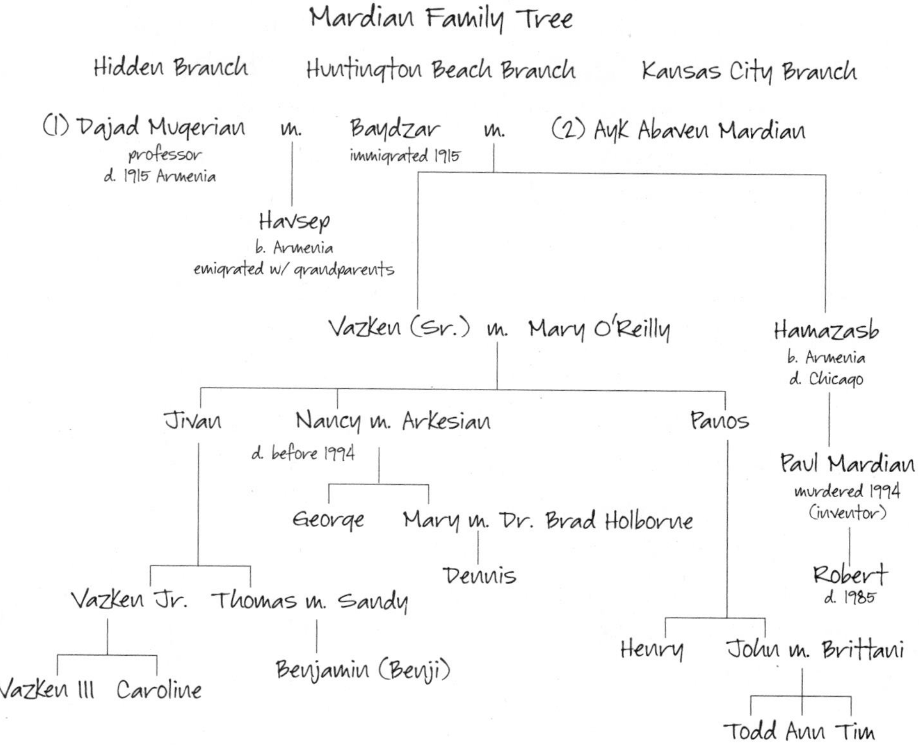

magazine that I found at Vaz's. It's called *Binding Hearts.*" Alex told them about the ad Paul Mardian had placed there. "Now that we know about Mugerian, we ought to be able to put down the outline of the puzzle, anyway."

"Yeah," Briggie said. "I'll bet Father Ghazarian would know about it. He's the priest. He was very sad about the antiquities being stolen. I guess Paul wrote, informing him about the bequest."

"Okay," Alex said. "Let's start a list. Number one: Talk to Father Ghazarian about Armenian forums—groups, publications, that sort of thing. Ask him if he knows of any Mugerian families in the

Southern California area. It makes sense that they live around here, and that's how this Leon knew about the California Mardians."

Richard mused. "You know, when I was in Paul's office, he had some magazine covers framed. *Fortune, Business Week,* that sort of thing. They all had his picture on the front when he made his first billion from the pop-top patent."

"Hmm," Briggie commented. "That must have been galling to this Mugerian dude. I wonder if he's the kind of guy who thinks the world owes him a living."

"He could have kidnapped Benji for the same reason," Alex said. "He wanted some of their money. The description the FBI gave me of the man who attempted to collect the ransom didn't fit any of the Mardian family. Neither did the description that Benji's captor gave."

"So," said Briggie. "He fits very nicely into the role of murderer, robber, and kidnapper. Doesn't sound like much of a churchgoer. But maybe Father Ghazarian knows his family."

"What're we waiting for?" asked Richard.

Chapter Twenty-One

Briggie called the Armenian Apostolic Church from Richard's cell phone. "Hello, Father, it's Brighamina Poulson again. I have a couple of questions, if you have a minute."

The priest made an inaudible but longwinded reply.

"I wondered, besides the church, is there an American-Armenian organization that tries to put families that were split up by the Holocaust in touch with one another?" Briggie fell silent as she listened to his response. "Oh, is that so? How fortunate! Do they have a publication or anything? Great! Now, just one more question. Have you heard of a family called Mugerian that lives anywhere around here? Oh, really? Yes, the surname was in the document that we had translated yesterday." Briggie signaled for a pen and was busy writing on Richard's probate file. "Okay. We'll give it a try. Thanks so much."

Everyone looked at Briggie expectantly. "Well, well," she said, "It seems we were right. There are several groups that meet at the church. One of them is an Armenian cultural preservation society. They meet tomorrow night. At the moment, they're working on presenting a white paper to The Hague on war crimes. Whoever stole that journal could surely use it as evidence. It's pretty lurid. They may be tempted to bring it to the group."

"Great!" said Alex. "You and I can turn up at the meeting tomorrow night. Now what about the Mugerians?"

"He said he knows of an old lady by that name. She has osteoarthritis and is a shut-in. He is going to try to get her address and phone number for us. He doesn't know her well, because she doesn't come to church."

"And the newsletter or whatever?" Richard asked.

"They do have one. It's published out of Chicago by some eccentric old widow. But everyone around here seems to subscribe. It's just what we thought—a surname exchange and forum for inquiries about family members. The magazine that Alex saw at Vaz's."

"Well," said Richard, "I'd say that was a good day's work. I'm ready for breakfast."

"Then," announced Alex, "I think Briggie and I should drive over to Mary's and give her the translation. At least she can have that, even if the journal's lost."

"And we can tell her about the meeting tomorrow night," said Briggie, satisfaction showing in her seamed face.

They decided to eat at a pastry shop Briggie had spotted on the boulevard. She insisted on calling Daniel to join them after Alex had her shower.

As they walked out into the light chill of the morning, Alex related her encounters with George and Vaz and her suspicions of each.

"Sounds like nothing more than flaming hormones to me," said Briggie. "I think this Mugerian connection sounds more solid."

"But how would anyone outside the family know about the journal? And it's written in Armenian, for heaven's sake. Besides that, I forgot to tell you, Henry's gone missing. The FBI have put out an APB. They're sure he's behind everything."

The pastry shop was on the second floor of a skateboard shop. It was very European, with a spectacular view of the ocean. Alex ordered hot chocolate with whipped cream and an order of French toast. She hadn't eaten much the night before and was starving.

"How's your arm, Alex?" Daniel asked as they perused the menu.

"I'm great," she reassured him. "Painkillers are working just fine."

"Are you really up to this visit to Mary? You're looking really pale."

He insisted on thinking she was made of glass.

"I'm going, Daniel," she said, trying not to snap at him.

He sighed. Alex ordered more hot chocolate. As far as she was concerned, chocolate was capable of making her fit for just about anything.

Daniel then turned to his father. "How about a drive down the coast this morning? There's an old Spanish mission in San Juan Capistrano that I'd like to see while I'm here. Let Alex and Briggie go to Mary's. If we all descend on her, she'll feel like she's been invaded."

"But I'm part of the team!" Richard protested.

"Richard, dear," said Briggie, "go with your son. He's feeling left out. And he's right about descending on poor Mary."

Her fiancé acquiesced less than graciously.

Mary was very happy to see Alex and Briggie. There was no evidence that her husband, Brad, was anywhere around, which was fine with Alex. Dennis was in bed, still sick.

"We brought you a copy of the journal translation and the copy that Alex made of the original," Briggie said. "The original was stolen when Alex was shot. Did you know that?"

"I heard. I can't figure out who would do such a thing, but I'm brokenhearted about it." She paused. Then she seemed to force a grin.

"But it's sure not your fault. And it's great news that you have another copy. And you got it translated? How exciting!" The little woman was dressed in aqua lounging pajamas with her hair artfully arranged in a French twist. With makeup on, she looked more her young age than she had the last time they saw her. Alex wondered if she was expecting someone.

They went into a small raspberry-colored room with white trim and white furniture. "This is my place. Or was. I move out tomorrow to Uncle Jivan's. We're going to keep one another company during our divorce proceedings. Janet isn't too happy about being kicked out, but I suspect she has a lover salted away somewhere. She's about thirty years younger than Uncle."

Briggie handed her the papers they had brought. "You might not want to read that on a full stomach. Your great-grandmother talks about the Armenian Holocaust in language that isn't too pretty."

As Mary read the translation, Alex noticed a copy of *Binding Hearts* on her coffee table. It was an earlier edition than Vaz's. Picking it up, she found that it also had Paul's ad in it. There were also spotlight features on several Armenian families. She wondered if they had done a feature on Paul Mardian at some point.

"This is rather sobering," Mary said of the journal. "My poor great-grandmother! Can you imagine living in a cave in the mountains?"

"Have you ever heard of her first husband's family? The Mugerians?"

Mary kept her eyes on the document, still reading. "Should I have?"

"It's just kind of a coincidence that that was the name of the genealogist who connected Paul with your family."

She looked up at this. "Really? How odd! He knew our family?"

"Yes. That's why I wondered if you'd heard of him."

"Never, I'm afraid. No one by that name goes to our church."

"There's a meeting tomorrow night at the church," Briggie told her. "It's a committee that's collecting accounts of atrocities against the Armenians to present to The Hague. You've got some good evidence there."

Alex added, "I wish we knew who stole that journal. It just doesn't make any sense. Did anyone in your family know about it?"

"Henry had heard of it from his father, Panos. He kept trying to convince me to give it to him. He wants to make a name for himself in these genocide studies, as you probably gathered."

"He didn't ever read it?"

"No. Aren't I mean? I would have let him translate it long ago, but he's so sneaky. I was afraid he would submit it under his name to that society you were telling me about. Now, that makes me sound petty. But my grandfather did leave it to me. I've always thought of it as my treasure."

"I understand," Briggie told her. "I have some things like that in my family. Some pioneer journals. That's why I feel so bad about your loss."

"It just doesn't make any sense," Alex said.

"Have the FBI investigators made any progress finding Benji's kidnapper?" Mary asked.

"No. But the descriptions they got eliminated Brad and Janet, unless they hired it done."

"Brad wouldn't hesitate to hire it done. That's one reason I'm moving out tomorrow. I really think he did it, though we can't prove it."

"We're working on a theory," Briggie said. "We'll let you know." She stood. "Now we'll get out of your hair. You're obviously expecting company."

"Just one more thing, Mary," Alex said, "Did Benji ever show you the little figurine that Jivan gave him?"

"Yes, he did, now that you mention it. I was excited when Uncle Jivan told me that the collection was coming to our church. Benji knew I would be, too. I'm the only one in the family who attends. Even Henry only goes to those genocide meetings."

"Did Benji show it to Henry, do you know?"

"Yes. Henry was furious when Uncle told him that the antiquities were going to the church. He thought they should stay in the family. He was so angry that I really, really think he killed Paul Mardian and stole them. I mean, who else could it be?"

"There is actually another suspect," Briggie said. "Although the police agree with you."

"Really? I had no idea! Who is it? Not another family member, I hope."

"A very distant family member," Alex's partner said. "From the Mugerian branch of the family. It tells about them in that journal."

Mary examined the paper in her hand, reading it once more. "A descendant of Baydzar and her first husband? A child that got left in Armenia? That's kind of a long shot. How on earth do you know he wasn't killed in the genocide?"

"We don't," Alex said, firmly stepping on Briggie's toe. "That's just Briggie's pet theory. She's prone to them. But it's not even solid enough to take to the police." Alex didn't know why, but she felt that with all the strange things happening, it would be best not to drag their theories into the mix.

When they left Mary's, Briggie said, "Call Agent Green on your cell phone. We haven't told him about the Mugerians yet."

Agents Green and Bailey met Alex and Briggie in the downstairs foyer of the Hyatt Regency. Alex left it to Briggie to tell them of the contents of the journal and their suspicions about the Mugerian clan.

She was still prone to sudden bouts of exhaustion and had to work hard at not slipping off the couch and onto the floor during the conversation. Perhaps it was because she was tired, but for the first time since her sobbing session on Vaz's shoulder, she began to doubt that she would be able to fix things with Charles. Missing him had been an actual physical pain, and now it grew almost unbearable.

"We think a descendant of this Havsep (Briggie showed them her descendancy chart) is Leon Mugerian, the 'genealogist' who told Paul Mardian about these Huntington Beach Mardians. He could have killed Paul Mardian for the artifacts. He could have kidnapped Benji for the money," Briggie said.

The agents agreed with the kidnapping accusation, but they favored Henry for the murder and the theft of the journal. Alex heard this discussion as though it were coming from a long way off.

The agents finally left, having received an urgent lead on Henry's whereabouts. His car was reported as being in a mall parking lot in the San Fernando Valley. Briggie took one look at Alex and said, "You need a nap. We haven't heard back yet from Father Ghazarian. I need to call him again. He only has Richard's cell number. When I get something solid, I'll wake you up. We can take the van and go visit her."

Briggie didn't usually fuss over her, but Alex was glad for the chance to take a nap. Now that she looked past her initial euphoria at finding the Mugerian name, it sounded like a terrible long shot. A little old lady was not who they were looking for. She was not only tired but dispirited. It occurred to her that she should have had another cup of hot chocolate. It had been the European kind—bittersweet. Her favorite.

Alex didn't just fall asleep, she plunged. But it wasn't a peaceful nap. She dreamt of Turks chasing her with curved scimitars. She was awakened by the phone.

A raspy, whispered voice said, "If you and your partner want to get the journal back, meet me in the gazebo on Cliff Drive in Laguna tonight at eleven. Bring five thousand dollars cash. The old guy should be good for it." The receiver buzzed in her ear.

She lay flat in bed, her heart pounding as though she'd just finished a full set of tennis with Charles. It was like something that would happen in the movies. But it meant that *they must be on the right track.*

She called Briggie in her room, but her friend wasn't there. Still not fully awake, she went into the bathroom and stuck her whole head under the bathtub faucet. Since she had given up coffee, this seemed to be the only thing that would bring her around when she was really exhausted. Slowly, she allowed the water to get colder and colder. Finally, scalp tingling, she grabbed blindly for a towel and rubbed her head as briskly as she could with her good arm. As she ran a comb through her tangles, her head cleared. She decided that the prudent thing to do was to contact Agents Green and Bailey. For all she knew, that could have been Henry on the phone.

She took the agents' card out of her carryall and placed a call to headquarters. Waiting impatiently to be patched through to their radio, she dumped out her bag and began to sort through the contents, throwing away gum wrappers and useless receipts.

"Bailey," she heard suddenly.

"Agent Bailey, this is Alex. I just got a call from someone who says he has the journal and wants me to meet him at the gazebo on Cliff Drive in Laguna tonight along with five thousand dollars. Either he was Henry, or you're looking for the wrong person."

"This lead we had on Henry's car is turning into a dead end. According to witnesses, the car has been here for over twenty-four hours. Looks like it was ditched here. So, we'll be heading back. What time does this guy propose meeting you?"

Alex told him. "Eleven P.M., and I don't know where this place is."

"We'll take care of it. Don't you go anywhere near there. He's probably going to be hiding in the landscaping with a gun to take you out for sure this time."

"Well, at least we know we're on the right track."

"Sure sounds like it. Are you sure it was a man on the phone? What did his voice sound like?"

"Well, I can't be positive. Someone was disguising his voice."

"Okay, then. We'll get on it. Take care of yourself. He obviously knows where to find you."

Chapter Twenty-Two

As her hair air dried, Alex managed to dress herself in clothes that would be acceptable to a little old lady—her sunset-colored gauze skirt and long-sleeved T-shirt—and replaced her sling. She clipped her cell phone to the waistband of her skirt so she wouldn't need her carryall.

Looking out her patio window, she noted that fog had rolled in. She couldn't even see the ocean. And, except for her early morning stroll, she hadn't spent a second on the beach yet. With her injury, swimming in the surf was out of the question, but she did hope the good weather would come back. She wanted at least one day in the sun.

There was a soft knock on the door. Briggie stood there in her navy polyester suit. She had apparently followed the same reasoning process about the visit as Alex.

"How's your arm?"

"Nearly good as new. Did you get the info from the priest?"

"I sure did. But first, we're going to eat some lunch. Half your problem is that you haven't been eating regular."

"Where's Richard?" Alex asked.

"I don't know. I expect he was coerced into going out to lunch with Daniel and the kids."

"So where does this old lady live?"

"Santa Ana. That's where the jail was. It's not a real nice part of town, I'm warning you."

After eating hamburgers in the hotel coffee shop, during which time Alex told Briggie about the anonymous phone call and the instructions to leave it up to Green and Bailey, they set out with the map from the concierge and an additional warning from him. Alex was very glad that the van was ordinary and not especially tempting to car thieves, especially when they got to their address. It was a very run-down, green stucco apartment building with rusting wrought iron railings and a burned out lawn.

In answer to their knock on the door of the second floor apartment, a gravelly voice called out, "Come in! It's open!"

A small, wrinkled lady with silver hair pulled tightly back into a clip sat in a recliner. She looked up at their entrance. On the wall behind her hung a wicked-looking curved sword. In her lap was Baydzar Mardian's missing journal.

Briggie and Alex exchanged glances. They had planned strategy on the way over. They were just two innocent genealogists.

"Hello, Mrs. Mugerian. I'm Brighamina Poulson, and this is my business partner, Alex Campbell. Father Ghazarian gave us your name. We're genealogists."

The woman looked at them, suspicion bright in her little brown eyes. "What do you want with an old woman?"

"Actually," Alex improvised, "we're doing an article for *Binding Hearts* magazine on the Mugerian family. We just have a few questions for you."

Mrs. Mugerian seemed to accept this as her due. "Hmph. It's

about time that publication focused on some ordinary Armenians. Not that we're ordinary. We have some pretty hair-raising stories to tell about the Holocaust, I can tell you!" While saying this, she tapped the journal in her lap with a fingertip.

"Were you born in Armenia?" Briggie asked as they settled on a lumpy red couch.

"No. My parents got out in 1915 when the genocide was just getting underway. I was born five years later."

"And you married a Mugerian? When did they come over?"

"They suffered through the worst of it. My husband, Havsep, was just a boy. He actually saw his father's tongue cut out and a bayonet stuck through his middle when he was only two. He remembered it until the day he died, two years ago. They burned the soles of Havsep's feet and left him alone and screaming with all that blood and gore until his mother came in from the fields."

Havsep, Baydzar's first baby. "How horrible!" Alex exclaimed. "He must have been scarred for life!"

"In his body and in his mind. His mother, Baydzar, took him to live in a cave with his father's parents for safety. They left the farm untended. That was a mistake. Those blood-sucking Mardians took it over! And then one of their sons married Baydzar and wanted to take Havsep away from his family to America!"

The woman had become terribly worked up. Alex and Briggie exchanged a glance. *So there was bad blood between the Mugerians and the Mardians from way back in the old country.* That made it even more likely that Leon was the murderer and the kidnapper.

"What is that book in your lap?" Alex asked.

"It's Baydzar's journal. My son's girlfriend lent it to me. She thought I might want to read about my husband's childhood."

Alex's thoughts collided with a crash, and everything she thought she had understood broke into pieces. Mary! Mary and Leon. Oh, glory, as Briggie would say. They hadn't even considered that a female Mardian could be part of the picture. Had Mary shot her? Or was it Leon? She probably told him she was getting the journal translated. Maybe he could read Armenian. His mother could, obviously. If so, he knew that it would point to him as the "genealogist." And possible murderer.

"Where did your son's girlfriend get it?" Briggie asked casually, but Alex knew that her thoughts had run along the same path.

"Oh, there's kind of a library of old records like this at the Armenian church. She found it there. She belongs to a group that is trying to put together something to send to The Hague so that the world will finally believe that the Turks committed genocide. All a waste of time. Nobody in this comfortable country wants to think about atrocities."

So she didn't know that Leon's girlfriend was descended from a Mardian. Did Mary know about the bad blood between the families? Was she in danger from Leon Mugerian?

Alex's mind was racing so fast that she didn't hear the door open.

"Who's this, Ma?" a man asked.

Alex spun around and saw a short, wiry man who was very good-looking in a wild, Heathcliff sort of way. *Leon.*

"Oh, they're some genealogists who are doing an article on the Mugerians. For that magazine. You know, something about broken hearts . . ."

"What'd you tell them, Ma?"

Evidently something in his tone conveyed danger, for Mrs. Mugerian cringed in her recliner. Leon was staring at Alex's sling. His eyes were as hard and black as coal.

"I was just telling Baydzar's story. You knew Mary lent this to me. Did you know your father had to live in a cave after his father was killed?"

"Yeah. I read it a while back." Leon walked over to Alex and, seizing her wounded arm, stripped off the sling and then tore at the bandage until her stitches were revealed. "I thought you were finished off!" he said. "That stupid woman, giving you that journal to copy!"

"You missed something," Alex said. "There was another copy, and now the FBI has it."

He sneered. "You're bluffing. Mary has it. The FBI knows nothing about me. They think it's the Mardians who have turned on each other. And after tonight, they'll be certain."

Alex bit her lip. She had absolutely no doubt that he was planning something dire for poor Mary as well as for them. She recognized the harsh voice of her caller.

Her arm had begun to throb. Leon picked up a cigarette butt from a nearby ashtray and smeared spent ash on her wound. Then he used both thumbs to grind it in between the stitches. Alex clamped her teeth so she wouldn't scream at the pain.

"We've got backup," Briggie told him. "If you don't let us leave, young man, you're going to find yourself in a very nasty mess."

Leon removed an automatic pistol from under his shirt and waved it at them. His mother watched the whole procedure with terror in her eyes.

"Ma's room," the man said.

"You're not going to shoot them, Leon! The neighbors will hear, and there will be no end of trouble!" his mother warned.

"I'm just stashing them here until dark, Ma. Don't worry, I'll do my dirty work elsewhere. It's going to be a very busy night." With his gun still pointed at Briggie and Alex, he groped on top of the bookcase, bringing down a wooden box. "You can have the coins to look at if you promise not to interfere."

Mrs. Mugerian's terrified eyes lit with pleasure.

The antiquities!

Alex followed Briggie through the doorway into a darkened room that smelled like dirty laundry. Opening a drawer in the bureau, Leon began rooting around among the miscellanea, presumably to find something to bind them with. *It was now or never.*

Alex moved quickly to his side and gave a swift karate chop to Leon's wrist. It jolted her wounded arm to the shoulder socket, but it was sufficient to make Leon drop the gun with a curse. Before he could react, she hiked up her skirt and kick-boxed him with strength born of terror. Her blow landed in his solar plexus and sent him to the floor. Alex grabbed the gun from the drawer where it had fallen. She knew she couldn't possibly shoot anyone, but she held it out straight, gripping the barrel with both hands like she had seen Scully do on *The X-Files.*

"Briggie, get out. Grab the journal and the coins. Then go to the van and start it up. I'll hold our old buddy Leon here, and be with you in a minute."

Briggie scooted out, mumbling something about Alex lecturing *her* on taking chances. Alex's arm was already burning with the strain of holding the gun out in front of her. Leon's eyes were downright scary. They were what she imagined hell would look like.

He sprang. She heard the front door slam as Leon knocked her to the floor. She had to put up a fight to give Briggie a chance to get to the van.

Leon wouldn't have gotten the gun from her so easily if it hadn't been in her right hand. Curling herself in a ball, she saw the butt of the gun coming down on the back of her head. Her last thought before he hit her was, "Not again! Wasn't being shot enough?"

Chapter Twenty-Three

Alex had no idea how long she was unconscious. It took her a while to realize she was lying on the floor of Mrs. Mugerian's house. Leon must have thought he'd killed her with that blow. What he didn't know was that she had an extremely hard head. But, as she was surfacing, her cell phone was ringing. Every move was painful, but she managed to answer it.

Briggie's voice said, "Alex, Leon and I are both in jail in Santa Ana. Can you come and tell these stupid cops that I didn't steal those coins and that Leon is a murderer and a kidnapper?"

"How did you wind up in jail this time?" Alex asked, exasperated.

"Leon was chasing me in his car, and I ran a couple of lights. We were both doing about sixty in a twenty-five zone. We both got stopped. I thought it was my lucky day. I told them about Leon, but as soon as they called in, the cops found out about my arrest the other night. Leon was claiming I had stolen the coins. But since I claimed he was a murderer and the FBI was after him, the cops decided to take both of us in."

"Well, at least you're safe in jail. Tell the police to get in touch with the FBI, for crying out loud. Leon knocked me out and I'm still pretty groggy. Besides, you took the van."

"Oh, my stars! Well, I guess you'd better call Richard to bail me out, and Daniel to come get you."

"Mind your p's and q's and keep from annoying the police. Honestly, Briggie!"

"Well, I couldn't let Leon catch me!"

Alex felt someone enter the room. Looking up from where she lay on the floor, she saw Leon's mother standing over her with the wicked, curved sword raised above her head.

"Gotta go, Briggs," she said and punched off the phone.

"You were sent by the Mardians to get the coins, weren't you? Everything you told me was a lie!" the old woman accused.

"I'm a genealogist," Alex said gently, trying to calm the woman. "I trace family trees—"

"I don't want to hear any more of your lies! You're a Turk! I can tell! You have black, curly hair!"

"My eyes are blue!" Alex insisted desperately. "See? Look! Turks have dark eyes."

The woman squinted at her. "You're part Turk. Your friend took my coins. My Tigranes II coins! They are *mine*! My husband had royal blood. He was descended from Tigranes. If we still had kings, my son would be king of Armenia! I'm the mother of a king, and I'm going to kill you by cutting your head off! That's what the Turks did to us!"

Alex had no idea how to defend herself against this crazy woman. Her head throbbed so much that she was afraid she had a concussion. Her arm was weak and raw. And the room was tiny, with no room to maneuver from her spot on the floor between the bed and the bureau.

But I'm not about to die by having my head chopped off by a crazy old lady!

Closing her eyes, she hit out with her good arm against Leon's mother's ankles, causing the woman to fall on top of her. The sword sliced through her skirt, and pain stabbed through her leg. Using all her remaining strength, Alex squirmed out from under the woman, crawling to the doorway. Despite the woman's malevolence, she sincerely hoped she hadn't injured her. Then the curve of the sword caught her ankle, slicing her again.

Alex made it to the doorway. She struggled to her knees and then stood. With adrenaline coursing through her, she slammed the door shut and collapsed against it. Using her cell phone, she called 911.

By the time the police and EMTs arrived, Leon's mother was crying pitifully in the bedroom, begging Alex to open the door. Alex was fighting waves of nausea from her concussion, and her legs were bleeding all over the old woman's dirty green carpet.

She didn't even try to explain, except to say that Leon's mother was delusional. Then she passed out again.

When she woke, she was in the emergency room of some unknown hospital. Her legs were being stitched by a short blond man who looked like a kid in green scrubs.

"This is a red-letter day," he told her. "I've never stitched up sword wounds before. Makes a nice change from knives."

"What happened to the woman who did this?" Alex asked. "Is she all right?"

"Actually, she broke her hip and is on her way to surgery. She's mumbling about some king and how she is his mother and how he won't stand for it. When was your last tetanus shot?"

"I haven't any idea," she answered, weary beyond words. "Have you checked my arm? It might be getting infected."

"We'll give it a look," the kid said. "What happened there?"

"Gunshot. It tore up an artery. And then some lunatic ground ash into it today."

"Awesome! Anything else?"

"I think I may have a concussion. I was struck by the butt of a gun."

"That old lady?"

"No. Her son, the king."

"And where is he, just out of curiosity?"

"In jail with my business partner."

He laughed. "You've got to be making this up! What kind of business is this dangerous?"

"Genealogy," she said, heaving a deep sigh.

Before she could pass out again, she called Daniel. He wasn't in, so she left a message after inquiring from the nurse what hospital she was in.

Alex was fast asleep on her gurney when she was awakened by a tender kiss on the cheek. At first she thought she was dreaming.

"Darling, you look like chopped liver," Charles said tenderly. "Does it hurt?"

"As a matter of fact, it does. They can't give me pain meds because I've got a concussion. What are you doing here?"

"Daniel played the gentleman and told me about your message to him. For some reason, he thought you might be happy to see me."

"Oh." She didn't know what else to say.

"I'm to tell you that someone called Leon Mugerian is in custody, and Briggie is once again at large, threatening a lawsuit against the police, the county, and the state for wrongful imprisonment. Richard is trying to explain to her that he cannot possibly take on the California bar examination at his age. I understand they are engaged. Do you think it will last?"

"So, she got hold of Agents Green and Bailey all right?" Alex replied anxiously. She couldn't imagine what he was feeling so jovial about.

"Yes. How *did* you get these new wounds, may I ask? Daniel told me about the artery in your arm. He said you were at death's door." In spite of his breezy tone, a concerned frown marked his forehead.

"Concussion is courtesy of Leon Mugerian, who hit me with his gun barrel. His demented mother was under the illusion that I was a Turk and pulled this ancient sword off the wall. She struck me a couple of times while I was coming to. The nurse who stitched me up thought the whole thing was 'awesome.' "

"You can't possibly give up this career, darling," he said. "You could never bear the peace and quiet of being the wife of an Oxford don."

She blinked. She was far too out of it to ask what had brought about this enormous change in him, so she just said, "You don't think your attractions will provide enough excitement?"

"I don't know if you're up to a demonstration, but let's give it a try." He gently pulled her up off the gurney until she was cradled in his arms. Then he kissed her with a passion that made her toes curl. "Oh" was all she could think of to say.

He kissed her hair gently and then laid her back down. "Don't worry, darling. I know I owe you an apology, and an explanation, and the rest of my life to make things up to you. I've got my eye on a quaint little cottage on Balboa Island. The realtor gave me the key. What if I take you there as soon as you're feeling up to it, and we can have it out?"

Suddenly her exhaustion disappeared in a red haze of anger. "You've had everything your own way all your life, haven't you? You think you're just entitled to whatever you want. You can break my heart and stomp on it and then breeze in with a few cheery words and expect everything to be all right. Well, it's not all right. I hurt like heck. Two extremely handsome and very wealthy bachelors are showing a great deal of interest in me. And then, of course, there's Daniel, who keeps me wrapped in cotton and would never dream of telling me I looked like chopped liver."

"You're still wearing my ring," he said soberly. "And believe me, I know I don't deserve it."

Every ounce of energy fled. Alex felt as though she were completely drained. She turned her head away. She was staring at the water jug on her bedside table when the room darkened. The edges of her vision became black. Soon the light was totally eclipsed.

When she regained consciousness, Charles was holding her hand. His head was bowed over it. Alex had the sense that a long time had passed. There was an IV in her arm, and she saw a bag of blood hanging above her. Transfusion? What had happened?

"Charles?"

He raised his head, and she saw new lines in his visage. His light beard was bristly and his eyes bloodshot. "Oh, darling, are you really awake?"

"What happened?"

"You almost died, Alex. It was very, very close. If Daniel hadn't told me about that artery, you would be gone."

"What do you mean?"

"You were absolutely gray. You were bleeding inside. I told the nurse that you had been shot in your artery before this recent struggle. They rushed you to emergency surgery. It was touch and go, but they were able to repair the artery again. The material that they used to repair it before had come loose, and you'd been hemorrhaging for who knows how long. Your heart nearly stopped."

"Oh."

"Alex, my dearest darling Alex, I thought I'd lost you. I've been pleading with the Lord for hours to give me another chance."

"If you hadn't been here, Charles, I would have died. No one in this hospital knew about that artery repair except some ER tech."

"Thank you, darling, for giving me some credit. But going through this made me realize all the hell that you had been through the first time, while I was in England, lost in my pathetic little doubts. I swear to you, Alex, I didn't know. Daniel told me about all the calls to my rooms and the messages he left, but I was at Frederick's. If I had known you almost died, I would have been here in a flash. I would even have left my mother."

"But what about your doubts about the gospel, Charles? We can't go forward if those are still in the way."

"That's the only good thing about my ignorance. After my mother died, I was sure it was all a bunch of nonsense. But then everything got really dark. I was smack in the middle of the existential void. Life had no meaning. The universe had no meaning. That's why men pickle themselves in alcohol. To keep from facing those things." He paused to kiss her forehead. "I couldn't sleep, so I read the Book of Mormon again, this time praying the whole way through. God was gracious to me, even after all my pride. The great and spacious building almost got me. But I *know* there were gold plates. There is no other explanation for that extraordinary book."

"So you're out of the Slough of Despond? What about your family?"

"I left them my copy and challenged them to read it before they made any further judgments. Mother was cremated, and I left directly after the memorial service."

"Just in time to save my life."

"To be fair, it was Daniel who saved your life by caring enough about you to tell me everything you'd been through."

He bent down and caressed her hair. "I understand now what you mean about putting the Savior first, Alex. I needed to go through that experience alone. Thank you, darling, for explaining it all to me and for being so firm in the face of my doubts."

"I very nearly wasn't," Alex said. "I think we'll always be tested and tried at every level we reach. That's mortality."

He kissed her gently on the lips. "Now," he whispered, "suppose you tell me about these handsome wealthy bachelors who have been trying to steal you away from me."

It was three days before Alex was fit enough to be discharged. The sword wounds had become infected, and she was long in regaining her stamina. During that time, Agents Green and Bailey came to visit.

"We thought you'd like to know that we picked up Mary Holborne for complicity in Benjamin's kidnapping. Mugerian told us it was all her idea. He was squealing like a pig. She didn't know about the inheritance until after Benji was kidnapped, and she just wanted the money to be able to leave her husband and take care of her son. She thought Mugerian would marry her."

"How in the world did she ever hook up with him?"

"At one of those Armenian Holocaust group meetings at the church. From her, he learned all about the Mardian family. Then he saw some sort of ad in a magazine his mother had about Paul Mardian looking for his cousins. He knew all about how wealthy Mardian was and figured if he got him together with Mary's family and they inherited eventually, he would come in for some of the money if he married Mary."

Alex thought this through. "He must have been pretty thorough in his description of the family. That wasn't in the letter he sent."

"Mary confessed that she convinced him to go visit and take pictures of her family with him. Paul had told Mugerian that he was dying. I guess he liked the look of Jivan as head of the family and decided to send him one of his artifacts, telling him its history. He said he had many more that he would leave to the local Armenian church so that they would be able to see them one day. My guess is that Paul probably told Mugerian about his collection."

"Yup," Agent Green concluded. "Mugerian just happened to be raised by a crazy mother who told him he'd lost his birthright when they left Armenia. He was more than a little nuts about the subject."

"I was sure it was Henry," Alex said. "Or even Vaz or George."

"What's going to happen to Mary's little boy?" Charles asked.

"Mrs. John Mardian is going to do her best to take care of him while Mary serves her time," Agent Bailey said. "But I don't think he'll live long. There's not much they can do for a kid with that birth defect. He's already defied statistics by living this long."

Shortly thereafter, the agents departed, leaving Charles and Alex alone.

Charles was looking haggard from his vigil at her bedside. The nurses had brought in another bed so he could sleep in the room instead of on the waiting room couch, but he obviously hadn't slept much.

"This is the worst punishment possible," he told her. "Seeing you in pain and not being able to do anything."

"Let's talk about something else," she said. "Will you take me snorkeling at the Great Barrier Reef for our honeymoon?"

"To the moon if you like. Anywhere, darling."

"I've always wanted to see the Great Barrier Reef. And I think the cottage on Balboa Island is a good idea. Very festive and un-Midwestern. I think it will be good for us to spend some of our time near the sea."

"Where are we going to live the rest of the time?" he asked.

"It's up to you, love. Do you want to continue tutoring?"

"I was never really cut out for it," he mused. "I like the mystery and the hunt of your profession far better."

She laughed. "So does Richard. It looks like we'd better expand our company. Good thing we don't have to live on the proceeds! It doesn't pay well."

"Maybe not. But it does so enrich one's life."

"If one lives through it," Alex sighed.

"There is that."

Epilogue

Alex had to admit that Briggie's royal blue wet suit was sporty. Richard, however, looked a trifle ridiculous in his yellow and black one. Sort of like a giant wasp. She smiled as she watched Vaz giving Briggie lessons with the boogie board. She was a natural, as Alex could have imagined. Richard was still standing with the water lapping around his ankles, looking very unlawyerly. Being married to Briggie would take him outside his comfort zone on a regular basis, that was for certain. To Alex's surprise and relief, he had also agreed to the missionary lessons as a condition of their engagement.

Marigny approached her grandfather, had a short conversation, and then took his hand and led him deeper into the ocean. Between his lady love and his granddaughter, Alex was certain he would soon be riding the waves.

"How would you feel about living here permanently?" Charles asked as he lay on his beach towel beside her. "In that cottage on Balboa that I haven't shown you yet?" Alex was propped up on a beach chair, dressed in her jeans and turtleneck to cover her various wounds.

"I think I like the four seasons," she said. "But this is sure a great place for a vacation."

The sea breeze was stirring her hair, and she loved the feel of the sun and the rhythm of the waves. She was secretly delighted that Charles's lovely biceps were freckling. Nearby, a volleyball game was in progress between two teams of Mardians. It was the first time she had met the younger generation, and she could not believe how incredibly athletic they were. They actually had team T-shirts. George, John, Brittani, their sons, Tim and Todd, and their daughter, Anna, wore emerald green with their names on the back and the legend "Skin 'em Alive" on the front. Thomas, Vaz, and his kids, Caroline and Vaz III, wore tie-dyed shirts with "We are the Bomb" in black letters on the back. Henry was off at the church today, organizing the exhibit of antiquities that would grace it after they had appeared as exhibits in Mugerian's trial. (It turned out Henry had taken refuge on his girlfriend's estate in some place called Morro Bay.) Jivan was tending the barbecue pit, where he roasted a leg of lamb. Marigny was actually up on her board now, surfing beside Benji. Only Sandy was missing, at home tending Dennis. The espresso bar and surf shop were being managed for once by hired hands.

Alex smelled the lamb roasting on the spit, while Charles fed her succulent pieces of mango.

"It's such a shame about Mary," Alex said. "She had no idea Leon was going to shoot me to get that journal back. He had read it and knew it would lead to him. She didn't even know he read Armenian."

"She'll probably do a plea bargain. Maybe she won't go to jail after all. Don't forget Dennis. Her love for him is probably the only thing that can get her to testify against Leon. Kidnapping and murder. Does California have the death penalty?"

"It sure does. And those are both capital crimes." Alex thought a while. "You know, with all the nationalistic hang-ups that separate us, it'll be a good thing when the Millennium comes."

"I agree. Maybe in the meantime we should live in Iceland."

"Truly, Charles, where do you want to live?"

"How about if we take over Briggie's big house in Independence, now that she's becoming a world traveler? We can remodel it and get it ready for kids."

Alex smiled. "I like that idea. That house needs children. And it has a huge basement we can finish for Briggie and Richard to stay in on their rare visits to town. Will you ever want to go back to Oxford?"

Charles shrugged and his blue eyes darkened. "I don't know. We'll have to see. A lot of it depends on my family. By the way, where has your other swain gone?"

"Which one?"

"Oh, I was forgetting. There are three of them, aren't there? I meant Daniel."

"He's picked up a bikini beauty over there." She gestured with her head to where Marigny's father was rubbing suntan lotion on a woman who was, at the most, ten years older than his daughter. "You win some, and you lose some. Maybe he'll move to California."

"That would make Marigny happy."

Alex exclaimed, "Look! Richard's actually using his boogie board!" Charles took a pinch of sand and sprinkled it through her curls. He smiled his lightning-white smile. "Yes, darling. Happy endings all around." After a moment he added, "Except for poor Vaz. I talked to him, you know. I believe he'll always see you as the one who got away."

About the Author

G. G. Vandagriff is a native Californian who lived at the beach every summer during her teens. After she graduated from Stanford University, she moved to the East, where she worked in Boston until she attended George Washington University for her master's degree. She married David P. Vandagriff, and they raised their three children in the Midwest. They now live in Provo, Utah.

A writer since the age of nine, G. G. has published nine books, including the acclaimed epic *The Last Waltz: A Novel of Love and War,* which took her thirty-three years to complete to her satisfaction. In the meantime, she enjoyed plotting and writing her Alex and Briggie genealogical mystery series, of which *The Hidden Branch* is the fifth volume.

G. G. loves to communicate with her fans through her blog: ggvandagriffblog.com, and her several websites: ggvandagriff.com, deliverance-depression.com, arthurianomen.com, and last-waltz .com.